WOMB OF FIRE-FLIES

AMBIKA BARMAN

Invincible Publishers

First published in India in 2019

ISBN : 978-93-88333-48-1

Invincible Publishers

201A, SAS Tower, Sector 38, Gurgaon-122003

Registered Address: Opposite Kasturba Ashram,
Radaur, Haryana–135133

Printed at Thomson Press (India) LTD

For my parents,
and all those lives I have met so far.

Acknowledgement

"Never to be less grateful to your creators than your faith in the beholder of this Universe."

So, immense love and gratitude born out of thanks to Baba and Ma, who have raised, cared and nourished me like their own shadow in all ups and downs of my life. More thanks to my English Literature department in Ramjas, all those faces, who shaped me, showed me and made me fall in love with writing. While I am, will always be one among the entire family in IIFT, Delhi. Finally, I would like to thank all my closest friends for being there for me forever.

"After all, passionate writing is medicine to conquer all those pains, which existed and still exist within me."

Contents

Preface

"Womb of Fireflies" was never the first choice to name the title of my first fiction. Rather, all those times, "The soft joy of happiness", was the one. Until, I felt the utter need of saying it out loud that humans of "G-Plot", have lived their entire lives under the pain of in existential crisis. So, the womb is the creation of all those lives while fireflies are all my people, living, breathing and staying in Sundarbans. Though Sun and his light, is brightest, still fireflies exist.

After all, how many humans of this world, have lived their lives, knowing that a little island amidst the vast waters of Bay of Bengal existed. Those lives also had dreams, desires born out of their own vulnerable conditions. So, here I, share all their stories after all how far I travel, my roots will always be those green, mysterious land of Sundarbans.

While the sole line blossoming in my mind, all for my protagonist Alok comes from,

Maybe you are searching among the branches for what only appears in the roots – Rumi

REFLECTION

Chapter 1

As I, Alok's not so little daughter, saw the day signing off.

The other side of our window looked better as the last bit of darkness faded. There were no fireflies to belittle themselves in front of the morning sun all gone. After all, that's what the sun promises, to hide the weakest under his light.

Still, unlike me, those little fireflies hid amidst sun's brightness have always known their worth, baba would often quote.

While, to me, this morning of Delhi looked pleasurable amidst silence as each and everything like the soft breeze passing through green leaves to the noises of the crowd, none of this was there. Plus, my ears also got used to the sole noise, the frequent pace of air entering Alok, my baba's nostrils to pass down and expand his lungs.

But this sun of our morning wasn't as beautiful as the one seen by the Sundarbans. Our distant, and their own sun had a line between darkness and brightness as that fiery sphere came out of the sea, The Bay of Bengal. Here the entire universe showed signs of restlessness lingering between two things; the tainted yellow colored sun, which was pretty impatient to come out to dominate the sky above all those Sundarbans' natives and my baba, Alok when he was still a child in 1985. After all, the blue sky above them, wanted to express its language, which spokes about those versions of freedom it had, or has as neither Alok nor his home knew when their sky would scare them, and leave behind a scar forever.

Still, their glowing yellow sun placed amidst the vast sky wasn't completely free. Looked like there was a greater force hidden in this universe, which forced and suppressed sun's prior color ranges like the orangish undertones complicated with the soft touches of red as the dawn arrived.

While the other impatient soul was baba in this morning of 2016.

After all, the peace within him was disrupted, because the same collection of daunting stories baba told me in repetition never relaxed him, even how much of those he shared with me. He laid there on his wooden bed and stared blankly at the ceiling as he narrated those stories to me for the umpteenth time. Time stood at a standstill when he would zone out to the times bygone. I just sat there and listened. Listened to every word he said. Nothing was new in his words, but I hung on.

I felt like Baba beastly forced upon those works on me, which pierced my thoughts without my own permission. All the while his stories kept on revisiting my subconsciousness for several consecutive nights.

This entire process changed me. I could feel goosebumps enlivening on my skin all over. Yet as it happens in all humanly happy stories, sadness finds routes of escape through dreams. All of mine also came to an end as the morning light seeped through my window. I knew the wait for this celestial sphere, the sun, awaited me.

I could clearly remember Baba's words, 'What would have this radiance of the rising sun purchased for the natives of Sundarbans back in 1980s? Do you know?

I knew his answer. Even mine was constructed out of his monotonous repetitions, yet I declined to lend my voice as my eyes played the innocence of unknown.

"A soft joy of happiness!" His clear words grew louder as they came to the end of the sentence.

He never said that he missed those minute details of Sundarbans, something which he himself couldn't feel amidst the daylight of Delhi drowned in cacophonous noises. But I knew, he did. All along, he would relish his strong smelled cup of coffee, which would hit my nostril multiple times as baba continued with his endless conversations and cups of coffee.

"Believe me that our soft joy was in believing that at the end of sheer darkness there will be reasons for our breathing. Finally, there will be light. So, our hearts won't be haunted for another twelve to thirteen hours. Freedom will be felt, each one of us will be free to come out of house, free to go to work and free to dream. After all, Sundarbans never dreamed big, all of their dreams were simple, yet, filled with insecurities like the one borne out of past experiences of painful realities. Nothing concrete weaved amidst the darkness of night.

So, their dreams unlike Baba's dream, remain unfulfilled. All of those flickered away like smoke from the weak flame amidst the light of a sunbeam. After all, their truth was different from ours, all of us residing in Delhi.

So, for what impossible reasons?

Thinking and waiting for the expected, yet unknown to them like violent attack of the royal bengal tiger. While those cyclones which were predictable to the world, remained undated to them on the following day of its approach.

Plus, even if Southern Sundarbans knew that there was an approaching cyclone none of them would have felt more than an incurable pain. A pain felt, but couldn't be treated. Much like something tragic was knocking their door, and banging hard to open it.

But all of them, had nowhere to go as Sundrabans were stuck within the strange middle. As the Sun sets in, nothing is left, nothing except muddy waters and dark shadows of Sundari Trees as a glistening reflection with vibrant patches of vulnerable inhabited islands. Meanwhile, the brackish mud-dissolved waters flowed like a snake between the mysterious Sundarbans on both sides, moving parallelly. So, where would you run? How long would your feet support you in darkness?

Finally, where will your feet seek for heaven, the some amount of rest? His words illuminated the mirage hidden beneath his face.

While Hari, baba's father, grandfather of mine, would bore the same pace of rush while forming words into sentences. Those endless conversations would come from somewhere yet not take me anywhere. Hari grandpa was a man of lean stature, clean shaven, deep skinned, bald headed while his intense determination peeked through the sharpness of his deep black iris. Still, he was known as his identity won't or couldn't be hidden within the small inhabited Southern Sundarbans' island, G-plot, where he worked as a local school headmaster. And, amidst all of his stories, Baba would always utter what was Hari grandpa's significance in his life. He was sweet as nectar. As are the ones filled with more kindness within themselves who suffer more between the noises of loud and less kind hearted. For him, grandpa was a trapped soul, waiting all along for the miracles to change his space, not his little home, rather the entire island called G-Plot. While his soul learned to fit in temporary cages as for him it was an achievement, a little memorandum born out of adjustment.

So, during mundane weekends, Hari would often meet his friends, play poker as his lips would come close to relish cups of milk tea near the street corner. All along, savoring, flavorful crisps made of chopped onions and sliced chilies with loads of spices, then dipped in gram flour batter, and deep fried in Bengal's favorite mustard oil. So, the number of hot cups would come, filled to the brim in turn waiting for the empty cups to come back and replace it. While he and his friends, all of them altogether would continue discussing the intrigue details of politics, stories about lives at work as the sunflower blooming fields would transform into crowded places to chatter, and continue endless conversations. Hari was different, he looked better from inside, still when you go down the roots, they all were same.

All these men, his friends, whom Hari considered a part of his own family, would fill their entire day's labor within a brimful glass of cheap alcohol called the fermented rice liquor.

Then, those men would arrive home all drunk and beat their respective wives till all of them would accept that those women were wrong for questioning their habits.

Hari was different as his own moralities separated him from being there version. He was wrapped under his sense of cultured belongingness.

Humans like Hari, knew that what would have been better, staying distant from all these men as he himself feared absorbing their energies and becoming one of them.

Plus, none of them gave him peace nor the comfort of happiness.

Then, what would have stopped Hari grandpa from leaving all of them and finding peace within his own solace? Baba understood years later.

All of this was all in grandpa's nature that hated to escape the trapped cage of comfort for the feeling of lonesome without them. So, he would maintain close-tied connections with them. While amidst all those little instances, his naked eyes won't decline judging them. After all, Hari was human although how genuine he might be. We knew that humans made mistakes.

Still, his glimpses of clean-shaven face and visible signs of premature baldness reflected a transparent honest character. Rather, all these qualities increased, became more glass transparent as you find the man he was, with a deep straight look into his eyes.

While his masculine tone found voice in all those moments he left the clasps of his upper and lower lip to utter a chain of words. After all, who said that a bit of softness in a man's voice, made him less of a man?

He was blessed with a feeble voice, which sounded calmer than his wife Pranati's sleek high-pitched voice. Rest of the magic was done by the soft stern handsomeness shaping his face from structures to cheekbones. And, somehow all of him, made him seem approachable to the crowd. So they would come to converse, and in the process know him. Finally, with pace, his words of kindness spread like a wildfire consuming the entire forest of pain, where every particle was born out of fear, need and abandonment among Sundarbans' natives.

"Hari, can you lend me few of your Bamboo logs?

As, the cattle shed is no longer capable enough to stand on its own, all broken", Ananto could hardly frame his own words.

While his distress found expression through his weighed down eyes under the baggage of tears. Though, none of this was uncommon after all someone would always rush to Hari after an end of another devastating storm, whose hunger for destruction was no less than that of Hercules.

Hari had few acres of land blessed with green, high-shooting tall Bamboo grasses on the back-end side of his kitchen wall, and for his son, and my baba, all of this was his own Bamboo garden. Still, Hari grandpa would never decline to share those bamboo grasses as he knew Sundarbans fate. On an average, no one earned more than 30 rupees back in 1980s. So, bare to barer faces only earned to feed themselves, not a penny reserved for the child's education or daughter's marriage. Saved nothing, they lived like a bare stone all along waiting to either drown or come near the offshore. Then, there were unknown men, whom people like Hari remembered only through the glimpses of their faces, no name or addresses, just the one with a large beard, the one with the bare upper body, the one with transfixed eyes, and a black and blue checked loin to cover him from the utter name of shamelessness. Though, he visited Hari's home, his front-yard on daily basis to beg for few coins, all he needed was one proper meal.

'Don't you need sugar?'

As, usual baba's answer was no.

He always loved to take his black tea without sugar or just with a little dash of honey once a while.

While, baba's body was reclined on the blackish-brown painted Mahogany armchair as he again started soaking me under the warmth of his stories. Those little pauses as he waited to fill in his lungs with air came out as a bedtime fable.

So, in that afternoon, when your Hari grandpa came back from work, after fulfilling his responsibilities, all those duties as an assistant headmaster, his mother, your great grandma called him from the backyard. Believe me, he was still standing in the open hall verandah. Hadn't yet crossed the main door to the bedroom.

All of a sudden, his treks halted.

'Didn't Ananto owe you money? You know this right. Have you taken it back from him?'

All along, Hari could see the frown was giving his mother a mild cardio to all of her forty-three muscles.

'Ma, he promised he will, but he can't return all of it right now.'

His times are not as stable as ours. His income is irregular. The sun never rises and sets at the same place.

Believe me, this other day, our Ananto was grieving about his loss in acres and acres of rice fields as he couldn't cut all of it, himself. Unwanted rain found its way before he could. Hari's voice wanted to safeguard the oppressed, which wasn't unknown to his mother.

He wanted to uplift them, stand by those known and unknown faces. His heart wasn't lost amidst the darkness of the mysterious Sunderbans. It was still perceivable, reached in need, and invoked into a blissful delight.

But chains of constraint wrapped all over him, pulled his strings of freedom from behind.

No matter how much he wanted but he couldn't reach out to them in all their needs. Especially, due to Hari's mother, who was conscious of their past, all her decades of economic struggle before Hari was born. She would never want him to land on the same plate, feel their brunt, lose out everything in the process. And, her existence, her words were his major constraint.

'Mother, can you make some mango syrup, its already that time of the year', said Hari. While the heat was becoming unbearable as the month of May saw its own end. One spoonful of raw mango syrup in water with a dash of sugar would have shown more love to his body, inside and out. Finally, after having a glass full of water conjugated with mango syrup, he went inside to take a short nap.

The dials on the clock, had gone beyond the late afternoon. Nevertheless, he was exhausted. Why won't he?

He has gone up and down, back and forth to take classes of the senior sections and handled bundles of official files. So, till the time dusk dropped below the lines of the vast waters of the sea, his body gave up. The weather was poignant outside, wind rushed lightly, yet he could feel the gush of chillness. But this month of summer made this rush of air, coming inside from the open left window, make him feel all relaxed.

His perspiration from the entire sweltered day, found one route to vanish as all of it got soaked and absorbed in wind as a thin invinsible lines of vapors. While all of this made him feel better, after all that's how Hari felt better with the slight touch of cold air all over the covered flesh as it makes one human feel.

All of a sudden, he could no longer hear the noise of the Kingfisher as the Pied Cuckoo went ahead and overpowered it.

All he could hear, was the song of the Cuckoo growing in decibels with each new stanza. He always remembered his mother's words, Cuckoo cried louder and louder in the Sundarbans,whenever the thunderous rains were coming.

And, she was right.

The natives of Sundarbans believed more in the Pied Cuckoo, who was the messenger of rain than the existence of a metrological department. Fortunately, none of them had to prioritize their choices back in 1965.

The scene outside changed, his open window was no more about the sun coming to dusk. While the growing dark outside, created shadows of outside trees inside his room, which made his entire room slightly mysterious than before.

Rain? Is it going to happen? What is the date this day? Questions were rambling inside his mind.

While around the same time, his eyes narrowed down to the date mentioned with black ink on Bengali Calendar, made of thin pulped paper. The month of May while the day was 25th.

And, before his eye could transfix towards on the dark sky, peeping all through the window. All of a sudden, this calendar started swinging.

Finally, the rain started.

The flow, or pattern of rain was always alike in the Sundarbans as a time span of a few minutes was enough to craft big droplets of rain. After all, universe had its own call. The loud thunderbolt would scare the locals, Was it another warning signal?

As if, another baby cyclone was about to drop from her mother's womb, with an energy greater than their existence.

While, the Brocaded carp with its beautiful silver lining was living in dilemma, till where the pond's lining existed. After all, the water was no longer within the pond, water was everywhere, each part of the ground was covered in water. So, as the pond's height kissed the paddy fields with gentleness. Those little baby carps left no opportunities to jump all over its new unbound territory after all, the water equalized and converted them into their home.

Next morning the rain stopped, not all of a sudden, just after pouring down the entire previous night. Then, drizzling for another two to three hours before coming to a halt.

This entire scenario made the corners of his window half damp and half-dried.

Hari was still lazing on his bed, half awoke, and half asleep. When he heard the sobbing voice of Ananto coming closer to him, as if, he rusing towards him.

Hari could feel like the entire storm was within him, eating him, until he decided to breathe it out, share with people like Hari.

After all, he understood that something was wrong. So, he got out of his bed and came to the open front yard. Till, then Ananto had reached there too. He was standing right in his front with his pale face and bulging, weighed down eyes.

Is he fine? An air of anxiousness surrounded Hari. He read the look of apprehension in Ananto's eyes, which was much more vulnerable than the pain to describe him. Though, tears poured, running through his cheeks, yet, he couldn't shed those tears for long. Still, towards the end, his eyelashes glistened with dampness, which made him look more vulnerable to Hari.

All together Hari could feel the race of his own heartbeat.

Has he lost everything? How can that be possible?

Cause the rain wasn't enough to see the end of human. After all, what is stopping him from opening up his heart? Didn't he come all way to me for that?

While his friend, Ananto was filled with stories weaved out of painful experiences, which couldn't be translated into words.

Just like a Frenchman, who can't speak English. So, neither he knew how to speak in volumes, nor could he show what he felt like otherwise.

What happened, Ananto? Is everything alright back at home? Why aren't you responding? Ananto, could you at least respond?

These were the last few words of Hari before Ananto gave up, and broke down in front of him.

Hari Da, it happened again. This season, my farm was spread with quintals of rice covered inside the brown hull. And, this rain happened again, just like the last season. Now, my brownish-yellow Paddy field is submerged under water, things changed for me within one night. Until yesterday morning, this rice field was glowing under the beams from sunshine. All of them, were blooming with happiness. And, this afternoon, nothing is left except black, smelly waters, which has suffocated and bent and broken the stems of the rice plants. Plus, the suffocation of debt is choking me more than those plants could ever feel.

Bon-Bibi (The guardian spirit of the Sundarbans) has forgotten about her children.

Ananto lived five blocks next to his home. He was a small-structured man, whose entire body bore patches of hyperpigmentation. As if, the blessing of sun was in his brown color.

While, he had large, square shaped, rough palms, beak sky touching nose, and stubborn growth of hair around his chin. Still, the touch of Sundarbans lied on his nails, which were bloodily chipped and mud infested.

Still, the signs of weakness never peeped through his skin as his structure was skinny-strong. While his bone structure was quite noticeable through the thin wrapped layer of his own flesh. Unlike Hari, his belly was inverted, almost feeling his back and his blue-green veins flowed like channel tributaries of Sundarbans in solitude.

So, before Ananto left his home Hari pressed few crisp notes, all hidden from his mother's eyes as cordial support in his hands. Ananto never gave birth to sin. He wanted to repay Hari's every single hard-earned money but it was something that was not in his fate. Though, he tried multiple times, he still failed in attempts like the beautiful card-house hit by sudden gush of wind. After all, Sundarbans had never been his loyal pet, one who could love him back with same affection, eye for an eye. The universe knew, Sundarbans didn't need men like Ananto. But, he needed her for his own existence.

Ananto's had one married sister, who was four years older to him and lived few houses next to his home. Still, there was a conscious barrier all in his mind. He could never ask her for similar kind of help that he could ask from men like Hari.

After all, not because he was closer to Hari but due to his own sister's own vulnerable condition of being a housewife running a family on a single income, married within Sundarbans at the same time. Isn't this one strange world where the older widows had power, yet, their daughters and daughter-in-laws lived under darkness. So, it was solely Hari, whose door he knocked at all his hard times.

Mother might have seen Ananto take leave from my room. His intuition was correct as his mother was waiting inside the room, furious with anger as Hari had disobeyed her again.

'Hari, believe me child, you will become penniless just like your father.' She repeated the same sentence after every couple of sentences on how he should take care of his own wealth, how money never goes on the plants, how each and every single piece of his income was hard-earned. She wasn't less kind compared to Hari, still those feelings never evolved out of her. She compressed those feelings piece by piece within her, until she could feel none of it within herself.

After all, Hari grandpa's father was a fisherman. So, unlike grandpa, who was a government employee, his flow of income was inconsistent. Still, Hari decided not to argue with his mother, just like at all other times.

There was a difficulty in explaining the world of education to the outside world, altogether to people who hadn't seen the fruits of education and his mother was one among them.

Though, I never questioned your father, still it hurts me to watch you be just like him, who would love to escape from his own family responsibilities, uttered Hari's Ma.

Deep inside, Hari knew at least his reasons to remain, mum was different from his own father.

WARMTH OF HOME

Chapter 2

Alok was standing in his hunched posture and dropping shoulders. His not so fresh face gave glimpse of deprivation. And, his eyes were heavier, weighed down with the baggage of dream he saw last night.

His body along with his shoulder, carried the soft burden of inclined head towards his right. He and his anatomical structure, looked distorted, under a beautiful art of clumsiness, which told stories of him leaving his bed a while before the dawning sun arrived. Still, for him, waking up early morning was not new. He was used to an early routine since he was six. All these years he would leave the relaxing comforts of his cotton checkered pillow in a jiffy, except for a few countable days. On rest of all those uncountable days the efforts to leave his sleep behind, came from his mother. Whether he wished or not, he was made to leave his cringed bedsheet as the final bit of darkness was losing out.

'What is taking you so long?' Finally, Pranati, his little world, his mother's voice reached his ears.

'Alok, what are you waiting for? This entire universe to come down, cast spell on you and make you rise along with its own new expansion?

Your classmate's mother was right, you and your gang of mischievous boys are no longer becoming wise. Believe me, an epitome of sluggishness has engulfed you, where no line of difference lies between you and all of them.'

Alok nodded his head, though not to appreciate her choice of words. After all, he wasn't ridiculing her. His entire mind was absent from this present, one-sided endless conversation, where neither his silence nor his mind could symbolize, he was all there, all amidst this dawn, within a small island in G-Plot close to Pranati. After all, the dense nerves inside his head loved to play peek-a-boo all underneath the dilemma of whether he was half-awake or half-asleep. Still, like all human bodies, Alok craved for the bed, which he himself knew promised nothing except comforts wrapped underneath the warmth of love.

'Can't you see? I can't even start worshipping the Goddesses until you bring those colorful flowers, which bloomed to stay near the warmth beneath her feet', Pranati repeated.

'Ma, hmmm...'

He, little Alok, was blessed with beautiful, large eyes. Still, when those eyelids shut themselves, it felt, as if the entire dawn has been waiting to see those eyes after last night's closure. Meanwhile, he moved in slower pace, all easy breezy, unaligned, as if, he was accustomed to the salted smell of the mischievous coastal winds. So, none of it hit his nose nor bothered him like a newcomer.

After a few more steps in the right direction, he reached the second last step of the wooden staircase, where the pond water had already created patches of green slimy algae near the joints of the staircase.

He bent down to sit. While his upper body arched towards the front, his entire lower body moved down the waist, curving into squat.

The water, unlike the howling Bay of Bengal was still, and hundreds of water lettuce were standing calm on it. Until, winds whispered their way through the fading moon softly glistening on water.

Splushhh!

One splash of water was enough to remove dried pale discharge clinched from the corners of his eye, waiting to be washed and cleaned.

Finally, pure pond water dissolved all of it, and transformed into sticky Asian boiled rice water. Yet, the cold temperature of this water gave him chills of horror, made his ingrown body hair, poky straight all over his tanned flesh.

'Ma, have you seen the caned flower basket? I have searched multiple times, it's not here.'

Universe through his lenses of justice knew, Alok didn't search for it. The path of justice was longer, so it was easier to lie and work less.

On the temple veranda, Pranati's high-pitch voice was audible from the inside of cattle-shed.

Still, the cane basket wasn't there. So, Alok unlocked the latch, and pushed open the bamboo door.

The temple was their reason for existence, Pranati had told Alok. Unlike, the huge ones for public use, this was maintained for personal use, and this commonness lied among all the households in Sundarbans. Their baggage of wealth mattered less as whether landlord or tenants, if at all they could afford a home, one temple would be always constructed next to it.

Sundarbans celebrated their lives, bloomed like tangerines with faith from Universe that they won't be drowned, rather taken care like its own seed. While the simple difference was in its extravagance, architecture and dimensions, which will never be same for two families. After all, wealth has always found home in lesser hands.

All individualistic households owned a constructed temple. With a similar belief in fate, Alok's grandfather, Hari's father constructed one small temple in the north-east corner of the front yard, just outside their home.

The placement was quite identical to that of an enclosed Spanish patio. The difference was in its foundation, which was much raw than that of the expected patio architecture.

This temple was sturdy, made out of long bamboo logs, then shaped with roughly cut wooden planks positioned to form an inverted V-shaped shed. After all, this was necessary to beat the sun's burning heat.

Still, none of this was adequate to hold back the tremendous rain or an abrupt cyclone. Inside temple, there was Shiva's shrine, framed photo of Kali, newly cut picture of Bon-Bibi from the local Bangla newspaper. One of the low wooden bench was aligned with few more Hindu Gods and Goddesses. Still, the central focus of this temple was their ancestral Goddesses, Manasa, who was carved out of soft clay, painted with monochromatic shades of red and white. All together illuminated with subtle glow as the shiny yellow colored paper jewel flattered like pure gold around her neck. Manasa is the Hindu Goddess of snake. Centuries back, even before Alok's grandpa called this small island in Sundarbans, his home, Manasa was a tribal Goddess. Manasa was Kali's partial child who promised to safeguard all those exiting on this beautiful earth. Time changes people's need, so with time she positioned herself in every Southern Bengal's household. She looked quite similar to Kali in her ways of expression towards her own power and boldness but unlike Kali she did not carry a ferocious grip of beheaded fifty-one skull heads, representing liberation, letting go of ego, all at once from the cycle of pain, birth and death.

Sundarbans needed her, she was the sole assurance of their escape from dangerous snakes. After all, this land was filled with innumerable genus of snakes, ranging from pythons to dog-faced, Ornate flying snake and parrot- green shade of Spot-tailed pit Viper, water snake hidden under the depths of pond while the agile ones floated without restrain underneath the stretch of vast waters, Bay of Bengal. The dangerous ones were closest to earth's bosom, hidden amidst the high raising grasses. So, Manasa's hold on snakes gave her power to protect devotees from the mouth of death due to snake bite.

Still, Manasa was never their ancestral goddess, until Alok's grandfather, Hari's father was born. And, just like one amongst the bunch of little butterflies, she found place in Alok's home. Faith develops out of time, growth is a process.

Her growth amidst all of them, started from unbound faith residing in Alok's grandfather, and his wife, the grandma's heart. As he dreamt of snakes, hissing with poison or without for four consecutive nights. When after an old man in his neighborhood got a terrible snakebite as he was uprooting the dense spread of unwanted weeds from his marsh occupied backyard, yet for his grandpa and grandma, both of them, this was an omen, not a reflection of over-thinking sub-consciousness.

It's not a good sign, said Alok's grandma, Sundarbans and dreams seen in Sundarbans, had its own language for them.

When bees giggled and undressed the flower, they knew that the sweet nectar of honey was waiting for them. When

Sun smiled, their fear would evaporate along with sweat, after all they would have less to face.

Nothing will happen to me, Alok's grandpa promised to his wife.

Just call the priest once, to remove unwanted dead souls lingering amidst us, and then to get our home purified.

The following day, Alok's grandma prayed with all she had. After all, all she had was him, if he isn't there everything of her would change. So, she washed Shiva's shrine with a concoction of holy Ganges water, milk and no honey other than Padma. Padma honey was Sundarbans treasure as the local bees drank nothing except sweetness sucked out of soft pink Lotus.

Why Padma? The reason was simple, Lotus was pure, stayed everywhere between dirt to mud, still the filth outside could never merge with the beauty inside of Lotus.

She considered it a bad omen. Subconscious has a meaning, which shouldn't be ignored. That's how universe shared its stories with them.

So, the local Priest was called. He was in good health and his love for his body was visible through his bellied pouch. While his white thread of Priesthood tightened near abdomen, lingering loose near his chest. Still, he was different from his junior priests as his head wasn't shaved.

The mark of sandalwood paste found space between his eyebrows, splitting his forehead into two halves, with stories coming from two generations he had seen with age.

Under the shadows of his direction, Manasa was placed inside the domain, yet, outside the house. She would avert the snake from entering the home, had said the priest.

Alok's Grandma nodded with utter respect and humbleness under the veil, which covered her face, and her existence.

Finally, the Goddess was placed as per his words to guard their unknown future and bring peace.

And, all of this happened years before Hari was born as their third child.

Manasa became one among them, created out of mud and bundles of straw by the local artisans. Once a year, after worshipping her, she would be submerged under water.

Next year, she came back from scratch hidden within a new idol. Still, all of this was beginning as with every passing year something new was added to the room of Manasa, her children, her relatives and her mother, Kali.

Like when Alok's paternal aunt travelled to Kashi, she brought a miniature showpiece of Shiva from there. Alok's mother got hold of a few wax carved Kali sculptures on her way back to Dakshineswar.

Meanwhile, little gifts like conch shells or packets of incense sticks, ranging from rose to jasmine, came from relatives or others living in his neighborhood, whenever they visited spiritual places.

Inside, conch shell in the temples laid in variations like small, big, white, colored, making most beautiful sound when gushed with mouthful of air. After all, the existence of conch shell was required in each and every bengali household, cause that's how stories of roots and culture are weaved, and passed on to new generations. The natives of Sundarbans believed that sound of conch purified the air, and awakened the God from its sleep. It was believed that if God slept with the rise of the moon, then the other side of the world smiled with happiness.

God never sleeps, you know. I knew, they didn't.

Within few decades, the small temple looked congested as the new additions were added to this room. So, before the birth of Alok, it was rebuilt again, piece by piece with layers of bricks, one above another as the cement flowed in between with warmth to hold it.

Still, this temple, even before it was newly constructed, under the shadows of strong foundation, its wall has heard echoes of cries and laughter in silence like on the day, Alok's grandpa once almost didn't return from his fishing trip to the deep waters, another around the birth of Hari without his father, or that year when Pranati had her first miscarriage. The tales of laughter, joy, and soft giggles as Hari and Pranati's bodies finally became one, consumed each other, till the sunshine made patterns on their bodies. Then, when the tears of satisfaction Alok's grandma had on the day, her little baby boy was born. The temple has seen it all.

Finally, his eyes matched with the cane wired basket, he caught hold of it. He came out, tightly pushed back the door to latch it.

Meanwhile, the temple door made harsh creaks as sharp edges of bamboo's joint stems caressed each other. A different taste of architecture. After all, this door was created out of hollow bamboo trunks, dissected into thin vertical strips, then aligned into structure of ten to twelve columns with three rows. Sharp pointed metal nails hugged the rows and columns like a mother, who can't differentiate between her twins. The wick lamp on the veranda flickered with every small stroke of wind.

Will all of them, come this morning, or not?

After all, this was routine for boys his age, where each and every morning before leaving for morning school, all of them would collect flowers for the day's worship. Still, none of those flowers were wild as society never found beauty within the different, after all only one sorted layer was waiting to be plucked and dispositioned under Manasa's feet. Next, these petite boys would collect Bilva leaves, all born out of single branch in structure of trifoliate. All of their flower baskets showed skies filled with shades of rainbow, like colors of happiness, joy, all blooming along though they knew it was their last day on earth.

Alok with his gang of petite boys, made a game out of it—whosoever had maximum number of flowers and Bilva leaves collected in the cane basket, victory was his or hers. Though, none of them had nothing to present to each other as reward, still day in and day out they participated, and got an inner satisfaction of being something the other couldn't be. The little six letter word—victory—in itself was precious, a reward, as humans are born with a nature to compete against each other.

'Alok, show me your basket?' One of his friends wanted to see who had won, he or Alok.

'Not much', Alok replied.

'Rather, my basket feels light, wanting more, and hungry to collect more.'

As each day can't be yours or his, some days he would be the one, other days he won't be. Still, his basket looked colorful, with red hibiscus, whose redness matched the blood oozing from Kali's beheaded demons in the picture. This dawn he just remained a mere participant in a race to succeed.

Finally, all those boys along with Alok dispersed. He went straight to his mother, and submitted his achievement loaded within the cane basket.

And, within a few minutes, he would change into his shirt and pant, in case the brown mud caressed his clothes with love as school uniform wasn't still there.

'Where are you? Have you brushed your teeth?

Puffed rice and milk is getting cold, Alok, come fast', his mother's voice penetrated amidst the openness and echoed through the walls of the kitchen.

But, see the magic, his presence was no longer there. He had already left. Ran towards the road aligned to the embankment of G-Plot.

Then, he would run without the catch of breath, jump high to break the lowest hanging neem twig to clean his teeth with. Amidst all of this his fingers exposed the pale wheatish stem enclosed within the rough bitter bark.

This was his routine, brushing on the go. While on mundane weekends, he would brush his teeth with powdered ashes of burned wood, the one collected from the mud oven. Their small world didn't believe in wasting, so they chopped those wood pieces, then reused the ones burned to ashes. Unlike us, they fell in love with each simple gift of nature. Though, this sounded strange, still ages ago, before Alok was born, or even his father, Hari took birth, Sundarbans cleaned their teeth with ashes of burned wood. People preferred it over the more commercial piece of teeth cleaning.

Their eyes had learned to will for it that this wasn't harmful. Rather, the purest form of activated charcoal, could brighten thirty-two dead cells. Plus, this was in their culture, ones not found in books, still existed as all of them passed it on from generations to generations through their habit.

While he brushed his teeth with little twigs of neem, he loved to walk on the lose sand next to the line aligning to the borderline of slanted brick red embankment. After all, this has grown to protect them as along the lines of decades, Bay of Bengal also arose. The soft water, which ended their thirst, can also drown them. And, all along, Alok filled his lungs with the intoxicated smell of the sea, a bit light, different, as if some kind of peace was carried in it. Still, the smell transitioned as it intertwined with light, bitter-sweet smell of the pulpy white-yellowish neem fruits, which thrashed themselves to splitting open on the ground. While some others squeezed themselves out under the unknown feet. It was as if the neem trees didn't need those hanging fruits any longer. There fall was irregular, left and right, it was everywhere, bigger ones unable to contain its own weight fell before the smaller fruits. It didn't matter, either they came to sustain or fall against the adversities.

The entire beauty was in the color—Sundarbans had never seen a tinted blue, fading out as the day come to its end. Like always, the sea was messed up within opaque muddiness, quite exhausted while collecting and throwing silts. The water under the depth came out with off-beat rush of brackish tides as it hurried forward to kiss the brown mudflat. This was the same sea that awoke the red hermit crabs with its soft gurgle inside their hollow homes. All of it felt like someone had washed a mud-dusted cloth within a soap solution, where magical bubbles of detergent were everywhere. The wave ended its life, and moved back with a heavy splash.

The sea continued his life in and outside the riverine as small birds chirped with continues fall and scaled up in noise ranges. Suddenly, from nowhere, a flock of Black Cormorant, commonly called "Pankouri" around here submerged her feet under water to search for her food. The waves desperate to touch her feather and drown it within itself, weren't quite successful as the bird often shook water from her sunbeam gleaming black feathers. And, one of the birds out of all, couldn't hold on to a single place for long as impatience made her stomach crumble. So, no longer, she stood near her little ones. She walked back and forth on the mudflat, loose pebble filled alluvial bank that cleaved the disproportionate roots of the Halophytic Mangrove shrubs like her own little bird, who clung to her mother for support and nourishment.

To those roots, the mudflat felt like home, where they could spread from everywhere without the fear of obstacle. Still, the roots weren't determined. Why would all of them fix their path in one direction?

While the bird was different, she had determined gaze towards the rush of waves who brought up the baby fishes along with it. Still, her eyes would linger for her little birds, who played and chirped with foolishness in all few minutes.

Amidst all of this, her right eye twined with glow, little sparkle, which she followed with a sharp dive in the shallow waters to come up with feast. Her catch, one fish, wasn't big. Just one small Java Barb.

Still, all for this was for her and her little ones. While her little birds were excited, all filled with adrenaline to pounce upon mother's sole possession. The fish squished between her narrow beak. As, they fought amongst each other to pounce first on it.

Finally, her mother was tired, irritated, so she aggravated her upscale noise in anger. Still, none of this unbearable at least not on the face of the sea.

The noise mellowed out of the sea was rough, but nothing like what Alok had seen in 1976. Hardly, four years back then.

Till this day when he recalls what he saw through his eyes, rips apart his soul.

The lean goat's kid's head was smashed under the debris, and for him this shock was more painful than all the grieves dissolved within his tears.

While the shelter above them, the tin roof was gone. The harsh winds were not the reason behind it. All was within the power of those destructive stormy waves, who arose to the height of tenth and twentieth. In case, resistance came towards them; all that water arose higher and higher.

The dead bodies laid near offshore for days. While the rotten smell didn't bother those souls, who survived all of this. After all, they just wanted to eat, water uncontaminated enough to drink, and less mixed with the taste of sea, less salty. But every art borne out of spilled milk, can't be fixed with ease. Nothing remained for those poor souls, trenches of sweet water merged with the sea and its muddiness, so the brown earth of Sundarbans forgot what it tasted like.

Dead fishes within the pond, bloated up to the surface, giving the brown waters a touch of silver lining. Rice fields next to it, perished, crops laid flat on the ground, mashed, fungi-infested.

Still, Alok could only see those little beats that break, not the real marks behind the aches. The other side of Sundarbans, back in East Bengal, now Bangladesh has seen the land devastated, broken into pieces.

He was Alok, so neither his little age nor his mind, could visualize his pain. All he could understand, and remember was Baba's pain as he narrated those outline of stories.

"The communication wasn't strong back then, still natives of G-plot, were aware about all those ruined families in East Bengal, who came in unequal numbers, lost families, accepted new members. Those discolored faces had one hope; sole resilience to survive. So, with more hope, and less life left within themselves, they carried the left ones in wooden dinghy. After all nothing was left to shed tears for and reached here, G-Plot and I-Plot, in search of a much stable land. That's how those broken hearts became next door neighbors of them.

'So, Ananto Uncle came from Bangladesh?'

Hari nodded his head.

That year Bhola Cyclone spared no one. Still out of all those incidents, tragic end of his little goat kid stayed strong in Alok's mind. Except that, not a single detail bothered him now. The fear has accustomed so deep within him, so instead of breaking him, crafted his strength from there.

Alok was eldest out of four. His mother, Pranati was merely seventeen when she conceived him in her unprepared womb beneath her Marigold skin. Hari was older than a decade to her. Pranati was nine when she had left her maiden name to become Hari's wife.

When Hari first time touched the warmth between her legs. Her sweetness came out as nervousness, not the excitement which rips the soul with fire. He wanted to consume her wholeness, unravel her like a book, the one he has been waiting so long to read. But, she mellowed with pain. There was no consent from her, she didn't know what consent feels like. She accepted all the miraculous kisses, and love he gave to her. Yet the love Hari treasured only for her, broke and ached her body into pieces.

She doubted his love, will the pain come back, evolve more than her blood and flesh can stand. Months later, she knew someone was blooming inside her like the dandelions from the bright sunbeam.

The change was bigger, deeper than her words could describe.

HER MISCARRIAGE

Chapter 3

Hari's mother broke the beautiful news to him. The year of 1972 has just begun, there was no one except Pranati, Hari and his mother, all three in the house. Rather, Hari has just entered home, after sipping cups of black tea from the local vendor. Till his last breath, Hari won't forget the significance of that day after losing his first child from Pranati's miscarriage. He felt content with his ability to be a part of new life. So, he searched day and night for the unborn child's name in silence.

While neither Pranati nor Hari's mother was aware off his idle weekends, he passed in between flipping yellow pages of Tagore's short stories, rhythmic poetries, to just seek for the child's name, all of it hidden amidst the hidden literature. After all, he wanted his or her name to be different, unique, not tangled within the cacophonies of local words. Still, those rustic words only coming to his lips. The comforts of mind, has always heard the common.

Should I name her, Charulata or Lolita?

What if my first child isn't a girl, but rather a baby boy.

Should I call him Rabi? My Sun. Made from a piece of Rabindranath. But if he didn't turn to be a good scholar.

Was it a mockery of him or Tagore? After all, Tagore hated cramming factual knowledge. Wasn't he different from the crowd? How does it matter, he scored less or more, or if went to school?

He has given more to this world than taken baggage from others. He remained, will always remain amidst his versions of art.

There was a soft grin on his face, he simply understood the baggage of risk he is attaching by imitating a legend's name. The unborn child's name remained undecided in the forthcoming months like those waves, who have

touched ashore and rebounded back into its home—the sea.

Still, the eagerness within him, to name the child with something that felt closer to its heart continued.

While his heart pounded, waited to feel the new experience, unfelt before. The atrocious thing about Hari was that he could never see its aftermath, nor what will change after his child will be born. For him, this child was unplanned, sudden, as if, his and Pranati's conjugal relationship was meant to produce a child. Sundarbans made Pranati feel that she will never be complete without child conceived out of her own blood.

"I heard that you are becoming father soon. Your mother came yesterday with packet of sweets, tell her those sweets tasted good.

I can see your mother's smile as bright as sunbeam. Something, we all missed after your father passed away", the old lady in her nineties conversed for a while with Hari.

Hari smiled back to her.

His home, the land of Sundarbans called readiness for bearing child as an excuse to not bear one. Otherwise, the family was hiding unknown disease of the woman. Men never had issues in generating a part of new life.

Something that Hari denied to believe, though his blood was carved out of Sundarbans. His root was different, his chain of ancestors has stayed in up north, until situations forced them to shift towards the South near the border of Bengal. He came from Koch-Rajbangshi clan, an indigenous community located amidst the land of many, composed out of North Bengal, Nepal, Assam, Bangladesh and few parts of Bihar. Their facial features were hybridization of different cultures like Austral-Asiatic, Dravidian, Mongoloid and Aryans. But, their misfortune was not knowing the original roots of their existence.

“To know a person, you need to know his roots”, old ladies would quote once in a while amidst their endless conversations.

After all, roots were an amalgamation of stories told through exchange of genes and blood, generation after generation. Different versions of its decoded origin came up, few interpreted through historical scriptures. While rest were passed from mouth to mouth through legendary stories. Hari’s father claimed them as one part of human chain, who entered India from the Thailand-Vietnam belt.

Hari had different stories to share with Alok, Mongolians merged with Dravidians to be Koch-Rajbangshi three thousand years ago. The Pre-Vedic class division placed them next to Upper-Class Hindu Brahmins, labelling them as Pudra Kshatriyas. Still, the thick air hugged the past for the future to foretold.

“Koch”, the word attached to the Rajbanshi like two lovers. Among the sub-divided group of Rajbanshi, all of them originated from the Koch Dynasty of Cooch Behar in North Bengal.

Alok still remembered the joy in his Baba's voice, "The tag of Kshatriya, best warrior clan and the last one to accept defeat on battleground was them. The last one to subjugate themselves in the face of the outsider. Until they became a detribalized group owing to the better half effect of religious influences. They were most exploited and vulnerable within the enclosure of Kshatriyas. So, they gave up social identity to gain upliftment, their leader back in the 20th century decided to fall under a different caste to improve their condition, provide their children better education, and fill their appetite with fermented rice not praise. They were the only clan, who came down, while others tried to merge within the crowd. All this happened after the emerge of New India, when constitution was compiling layers of rules and regulation. The flow of new history washed away, their real stories of power and sacrifice, like the autumn wind does to its leaves."

The pale face of Pranati cringed with pain. When she ran towards the washroom to puke for the third time. The butterflies in her stomach felt like dying for peace.

'Are you fine, Pranati?' Hari shouted from the bedroom.

Hari has always felt lack of connection with her, she never outpoured her heart out like him. She always tended to hide herself from him, Hari knew that.

'I am fine, its nothing', she replied.

The way Hari hid the choice of unvaried names for the unborn child, Pranati concealed her morning sickness from him like the lush green Sundarbans forest, who tries to hide tigers under its shadow. Still, the world knew where it prevailed for life. Hari knew, she wasn't well, that she was going through something, yet from where the pain evolved, he wanted to hear from her mouth.

Was the pain enough for her to describe, he never thought.

She wanted to share, still she couldn't. Mother's taught their daughter what to share and what not to, the pain of childbirth was meant to be felt in silence, not to allure the family and make them be its part.

Hari's mother was calling her.

So, she finally found an escape route to escape from his questions, which she found hard to answer. After all, her mother-in-law in place of her own mother, told that certain signs she needed to hide, because there was nothing beautiful lying beneath its process. The advice would be passed on from mother-in-law to daughter-in-law like an endless vicious cycle. So, all women covered all signs of their pain, everything about the process, yet, called the final result beautiful, the little child.

The loose end of Pranati's saree was dangling like dandelions moved by the swift breeze.

Wrap the loose end around your waist, said her mother-in-law. Though, it was too soon to hide the bare midriff, still her mother-in-law made her conscious about her changing thick waist. There will be days, when she would tuck the loose end with so much tightness and grip, that the discomfort of her culture would overpower her pain as a mother.

The Rajbanshi child wasn't born, still he felt unwanted to Pranati. She was young to give an opinion, whether she wanted the unborn or not, she herself didn't know. While her cultural understanding painted a fence, whether to ask these questions or not, or should she keep all of it within herself.

The scenario would have been different, if she would have aged few numbers more, with time for herself.

After all, it was Hari's mother who wanted the little grandchild. Her intense desire grew more passionate, with passage of time as her husband, Hari's father left the universe known to her. Till her age, she has experienced all faces of life except feeling her past reconcile back through Hari's child. Remembering her initial days of marriage, childbirth and the family, who owned her.

While her ambitions died with her husband, the cooking recipes she tried for his apprehension lived passively, lifeless amidst the rough pages of her hand-bound notebook.

This loss of hers, also snatched her, dressing time. The plain white saree and a thin beaded thread near her neckline, was all she possessed.

"Hold her tight, the hair won't be cut straight otherwise", two widows held her within a rough grip.

While the oldest among the three, chopped her hair till shoulder length like the blades dissecting tree's branches without its desire. Next couple of days, Hari's mother mourned more for her hair than her husband lost while she was still in her mid-twenties. Her shiny black, waist length hair were the sole cause for her beauty. After all, of all of her physical beauty, it was her hair which caught Hari's father's eyes on the night of their marriage. Still, her hair paid the cost of his death.

Though, her hair was just a part of it as the colors which decorated her entire body like a goddess was gone. Basic symbols of Bengali marriage—a pair of red and white bangles, peacock designed gold danglers, long chain with intricately detailed locket, were all kept for Hari's wife. While her huge collection of red and Magenta silk sarees with Zari embroidered border, just stayed within her wooden Mango cupboard and no longer needed the white naphthalene balls. Within next few months, all of these sarees, piece by piece were replaced with plain white handloom threaded sarees.

Though, all along he was alive, and whenever she opened the cupboard, the smell of naphthalene no longer lingered, as if, it was her own body smell.

Finally, she was no longer needed, her existence became meaningless to this small island, G-Plot.

The marriage invitation cards were no longer meant for her as she became a bad omen to the newly wedded couples. She lived in and with her past, so the hope of a grandchild was the sole reflection to her lost days of happiness.

Hari, my son, this house looks vacant, she often said within six months of their marriage.

Hari knew what would be her next statement. Still, Hari chose to remain silent, the direct answer would have started endless conversations spilling into arguments on this Sunday afternoon.

Though he loved kids. The chubby four-year-old kid next-door loved to spend his evenings with him. Hari would often offer him two paisa tamarind candies from the neighborhood shop, which smelled like raw tamarind as it melted inside the warmth of his own mouth. Still, he didn't know, what it would feel like to see a child sharing the bed between him and her. Someone composed of his own blood, stole his features beneath her skin, all under the darkness of night.

After all, she was his first child. He wasn't biased, would have never unwelcomed a girl child, still from deep within he wished for one boy. The next summer Pranati lost the girl within seven months of conceiving. It just remained like a moth hidden inside the cocoon that never saw the light of the day as a butterfly. This miscarriage not only shook Pranati, but also Hari, who understood more than her what it felt like to lose someone of your own. The trauma changed the heart deep inside Hari, from the careless man who loved watching football matches of inter-school students after his classes at school than caring for his own fever-stricken wife at home.

All of a sudden, his priorities changed as he would rush back home early enough to check that she is fine. He didn't need to enter his home to seek for Pranati, because she would often come out with a steel glass filled with water in her happiness or loss. After all, it was her duty to serve him.

While Hari's mother sitting on the bamboo cot, the one weaved together with jute knitted rope, waited for him to return.

All along, her fingers crisscrossed like the thin branches of vineyard making love to each other, to knit the winter sweaters. As, Hari gulped down the water through his parched throat. 'Did you eat your lunch on time?' He would ask.

His voice sounded, as if, she belonged to him. After all the voice was authoritative towards her. But he wasn't as he was simply concerned after she lost her first child. He knew, she shared less still he wanted to absorb all of her, the entire universe of her own she hid like the seeds inside the enclosure. He tried to search for some exhaustion on her face, yet, as usual she looked more relaxed than him.

Was she pretending? He never came to know.

When the second unborn child resided in its home, her womb, Hari was scared about the way, the child might end up leaving its home, never see the brightness of the rising Sundarbans Sun, cause the way her last fetal left, the memory had always stayed within them. The constant anonymous voices dragged his brain cells until he drowned back to sleep.

Will it ever be born? The child might look like me or have big dark eyes like Pranati. What if, he had thin lips like mine which only felt completed with the touch of her fuller lips?

While the child resided within her like mother resides within her bigger mother, the universe. There were few more months to wait, until the child would leave the womb and be a part of his bigger mother.

During her time of marriage, she was thin, flat-breasted with no curves shaped like the dancing waves near her waist. Her face structure was childlike, filled with ignorance, nothing beautiful nor pretty. That's how the amateur artist, Hari's mother judged the priceless procession hidden beneath the common. While after marriage, Pranati's adolescence filled each of her structure, all of her own like her small breasts and dark caramel skinned thighs like the Sunflower who bloomed from every speckle of sunlight.

The past is gone forever, and this day she looked like one bronze Goddess with fat dissipated around her perfect places.

While her big eyes and sharp angular cheekbones like a boat's arch complimented her. For him, her phases of pregnancy seemed to be like the Harvest moon whose light blessed her clear face with a soft glow, until the child left her, withdrawn from her womb, the glow was always there. This aroused Hari multiple times. So, on days like these he would challenge himself to make his urges come to rest, not desiring to become one within her. After all, his urges only needed one imagination, the visual of the child within her for the rush of testosterone to relax as an unpleasant guilt.

To him, she looked no less than a Goddess nor her powers were as he could see her transforming into creator, the one he could never be. The version of manhood Hari reared, was unacceptable in their culture, but then he was different. He was more educated and used the power of critical thinking to differentiate between the glass and the mirror.

While Pranati was sitting, facing him towards the front. Her loose end of the saree veiled her forehead, as if, her dressing sense was meant to announce respect. Still, her face wasn't hidden beneath the veil.

All along, her right hand gripped the Phulkari carved fan to scare away those hideous flies planning to taste Hari's brunch. Phulkari designed fan was common in every

Sundarbans household, made at home with coarse cloth stitched together and embroidered with delicate threadwork.

While the handspun threadwork told stories from the ancient past like the birth of Shiva, his auspicious marriage with Parvati. This entire upper cloth base was supported with Polished Bamboo stick like a human backbone, which had aches and history written all over it.

She was holding the Fuschia colored Phulkari fan, a large painted Lotus was stranded in the middle of its design. While the sole difference was in its shade of pink, the Lotus was much lighter in color compared to the entire semi-circle shaped background.

Finally, the Sun was no longer in the middle of faded blue sky, shifted towards the right with the phase of day coming towards the end. It wasn't afternoon, rather late in the afternoon. While Hari relished his steamed rice mixed with Tilapia curry made with Tamarind. Tamarind grew throughout the east of G-Plot like an abandoned child of wild. And, as usual the food was served on the huge brass plate along with brass glass filled with water till its brim.

'Durga Puja is around the corner', the voice of Pranati came out with hesitation.

Hari understood her, the half-complete sentences were already completed within his mind like a maze out of the puzzle. The Sanskrit translation of Puja signified worship, where Durga fitted with Kali and Manasa, the Hindu Female deities who took pride in eliminating the evil from this Universe

'The monthly salary is yet to come', Hari responded.

As usual, she wanted to start the festive preparations before the month of September planned to end itself. Though, the dates on Bengali calendar wasn't as close as their hearts were to the festival like the await of Christmas for the West.

Hari saw, she has already marked the important dates on calendar with a red circle around it. While the color red reminded Hari about the exact shade of red, she wanted for her new saree, which she could flaunt with happiness on the Goddess's final departure, Navami. Hari's incompetent memory needed the validation of those circled dates to keep track in his mind. Still, the date of 24th March, 1972 was imprinted like a permanent stamp within him. His father was gone, no longer present to capture the image of his first child. Hari's father died in his mid-sixties.

I won't die so early, will await to see the glimpse of your son's face, he had said to Hari a long time back. It was like the long story which found eternal solace with passage of time. His death came as a shock to his entire family. The day before he left all of them to ride for abode, he ate the supper Pranati made with her own hands. He even pointed that the salt was less in the mashed boiled potato, which was spiced up with dried red chilies and shallow fried onions.

When Hari reached his Mid-Thirty, he developed one habit, a good one though to wake up his father somewhere around six in the morning. It was mutual routine between both, father and his son.

Until, one day of 1972 that never started for his father ever again. Hari tried for hours, slapped his red blood body for hours. There he was, his father with shoulder scratched and imprinted with marks from the wild tiger's nails. So, eyes protruded like a fork swapped on a cooked fish's eye. There was a look of horror on his face, even the curvature of swollen lips spoke million words for Hari to comprehend. His blue and white checked loin cloth was half-soaked and rest dried in blood.

While their little calf became the final prey for the tiger to take back inside the dark Sundarbans. As, the calf disappeared from the thatched straw roof enclosing the four cornered mud walls from the top. The gossip circled, if the wild beast came outside the forest, and wanted to prey over the little calf, why did he attack Hari's father?

The entire community shed their tears that night, less for his father, more for Hari's loss. The corpse was taken near the mudflat and caged with less-moisture laden chopped woods. Though, Hari never wanted his soul to leave this universe, take another form, rather wanted him to reside amidst them, all within the small island of G-plot. Still, the entire human generation came down to ashes, the pleasure, guilt, anger, ego all merged and spread on the brown earth. The death of Hari's father was heavy on him, difficult for Hari, but more difficult for Pranati.

After all, her eight-week pregnant little womb screamed for food; she satisfied her pain till daylight by just swallowing water. Until the sun drowned in the sea, then she could grab some boiled rice and unsalted mashed potato to follow her father-in-law's after death ritual. This was followed for the next fifteen days, with time everyone except Hari and his little family forgot about him.

This time the eight years old Raghu was attacked. The day was Friday, pretty much in the evening as he was grazing his fat goat near the tall, dense bamboo forest. The grasses in wildness, had grown few inches tall from the last monsoon. Raghu was sharing his short-stories with Arpan, his school friend.

This Math teacher is ruthless, gives all the sums for homework.

True, he is just lessening his difficult part of the task. As usual, he solves the easier ones in the class, Arpan added to Raghu's conversation.

While Raghu's goat teared apart the baby grasses from the roots, trying to grab as much as possible in one go.

Did you hear that noise?

The shadow Raghu saw, passed through the dew sprinkled grasses like a quick flow of wind. And, before, he could turn around, he was gone as the trauma of the horror resided within Arpan's heart. Raghu was grabbed by his neck and dragged inside the lush green forest.

HER BIRTH

Chapter 4

When the little child's month to leave home, his mother's womb, came closer. Hari felt a deep connection towards his belated father. The phase of parenthood was rearing the happiness of unexperienced relationship to him. After all, the magic was in await for the moment, once arrived all gone.

He recalled his own stories trapped within his head like how his father felt the day little Hari was born. The inside of Hari was like him, still he could never compete with his pear-shaped father, whose short stature, and temper aroused like the dandelions blooming with the news of Sun from moon, the spark was enough to lite the fire within him. The words came to his mouth but remained unheard, unspoken. While all of this suffocated him like the shut doors left behind with no windows, no routes for escape.

Why couldn't he have stayed for a few more months?

All those words ate him like the green caterpillar who feasted on the silk cocoon. In his case, these words sucked his feeling, poured numbness and tasted his piles of pain. Still, the answer remained unanswered. While there was another answer, which bloomed like one beautiful piece of rose shadowing Hari's painful thorns of unanswered questions.

"I have swirled Indian flag, circled around the entire school ground while this country payed homage to the brave souls after two decades of this nation's Independence. Believe me, I wasn't more than five." These were her sentences, all she could share with Hari on the night of their marriage.

To a simple question, when did you chase happiness last time?

Her answer was more of a little girl than his wife, Pranati. Still, Hari wasn't surprised, she was nine when she left her maiden name, her roots to seek place within Hari's home, his roots, which was never her. Plus, she became more vulnerable with a sense of hollowness swiping inside her as her mother-in-law kept her controlling with more stringent attitude. Her mind was confused, has she lost all the freedom with the phase of enlarging womb. While Hari's spine felt grandeur chill due to anxiety of the unborn, who was in its last week of creation, until it sees the light on Earth. The constant fear also bothered him, he had seen the end of his first child, the little unborn girl, whose cord of nourishment and oxygen disconnected as Pranati's right leg slipped on algae infested stairs, which connected the pond from the land above.

Today, he wanted to preserve this child, less for Pranati, more for himself.

The sound of conch shell, sandalwood smell of incense stick, noise of Holy brass bell bore enthusiasm as all of this welcomed the arrival of Goddess Durga. The songs of Durga Agomoni, were the little stories of Goddess narrated with high and low pitch tune of traditional folk music. The fable of Durga saving the Universe, fighting the kings of demon to save the Hindu Gods and making the demon realize his mistakes. Still this Universe, which gave power to the

Goddess couldn't witness the power of Sundarbans women on Earth.

While the air of this little island, G-plot was breathing the smell of spiritual love amidst the songs, taste of Khichdi Prasadam, human brows merged with black dot made of ash and homemade butter paste.

After all, this was the day of celebration while the air at Hari's home was filled with tension.

He rushed door to door, to search for the mid-wife as the entire island had only two mid-wives to save the mother and child from the mouth of death. On this auspicious day, one was ill and another mid-wife was delivering child from another mother, bringing her child to life without the support of his mother breathing for him. He waited outside the door, banging time to time, and prayed to God, expecting the other women's delivery to be faster, so she could reach on time for Pranati.

The child will never see the light of dawn, Pranati's mind rambled with unspoken words. Her mouth opened to scream, to outlet the pain, until it echoed back within the window-less room. There was no room to contain her impure body, which made the child beautiful, yet, not her. Sadly she was given no space inside her own house.

The sole place to deliver her child was the store room, separated from home as the cattle-shed came in between. The store room was just like her purposeless body, which meant nothing to Sundarbans, other than bearing her own child, which remained closed for years where one-sixth of it was occupied with broken parts of Hari's last cycle. So, before Pranati was made to enter, this room was cleaned and sanitized with disinfectant.

Finally, the mid-wife congratulated the father as she handed over the child wrapped in soft white cloth, and left with Hari to deliver Pranati's unborn child.

Pranati pressed her teeth together with utter pain, as if, her entire lower abdomen was cracking into pieces. She laid slumped on a bunch of folded old sarees over a thin mattress.

The mid-wife had reached her just in time. She moved her eyeballs from left to right to check if she hadn't missed any of the equipments necessary for the child to come out, but she didn't.

The white Chinaware plate with two blue lines circling its rim was uncovered, so it exposed a new steel scissor, mesh of cotton balls and a shady knife.

Pranati breathed, just keep breathing while the voice of Hari's mother forced her to push ever harder. She was in so much pain that all the voices were muddling in her head creating chaos like those different birds on the mudflat. Meanwhile, Hari standing outside the closed store room prayed for his child and wife, he wanted his family to be complete including Pranati. His mind was pouring negative thoughts, but the echoes of song played in the marquee close to his home, reminded him again and again that the unborn had his blood, blood of Sundarbans where their ancestors had fought single-handed with the Royal Bengal Tiger. This child won't fade out.

The child came out with every release of her Mother's pain. Finally, the little boy was cleaned of the last drop of her mother's blood, which he was soaked but surviving into. Pranati saw him as he was made to rest on her mother's bosom. After all that's where the entire universe lied. Gleefully his grandma played the conch thrice to announce the birth of the baby boy to the world.

He was healthy; chunks of baby fat adorned his body near the waistline. He was blessed with big round eyes, a black mole on the left of his chin, pink curvy lips and big ears like his mother, his hair all curled up like coiled telephone wires. His father named him, Alok, the brilliance of light.

Though this wasn't the name he had decided upon when Alok was still living inside his mother. Until the moment the fifty-five years old mid-wife handed him over the little child and his little hands covered over his broad long palm made him feel blessed. While the sublimity of his strong gaze confirmed that the name, Alok was a good choice in his conscious mind.

Alok didn't look innocent but his big round eyes gave depth to his honest behavioral attitude, all hidden beneath his marigold colored skin, or at least that's what Hari imagined. Still, Hari couldn't see his ambitious hunger, which made him submerge his Sundarbans roots and hold on to new roots for a better tomorrow. This wasn't even wrong as Alok was too small to show himself as he was, and Hari's biased eyes couldn't have foregone it.

Alok, this is your third time, you little piece of mischievous, Hari said with a playfulness in his tone.

His white and blue colored checkered loincloth coming to his ankles was again marked with patches of Alok's pee stain. As if, he marked his territory to remember where his home was. Alok laughed bluntly, looked like his heart was filled with happiness. His smile seemed like his father miscommunicated those words, as if, his baba wasn't scolding him, rather appreciating his deeds.

While entirely this one-sided conversation with mutual laughs once in a while brought a smirk on Hari's long, dark face.

You, my little child, such a raunchy one you are.... still you are mine, Hari repeated within his own head.

Hari's pronunciation without my English translation would have sounded distorted but this wasn't all together his fault. The Bangla language the natives of Sundarbans spoke among themselves had a colloquial touch to it. The consideration of Bangla as one of the sweetest languages was true. The Bangla G-Plot's people spoke didn't match with the aesthetics West Bengal's cultural brought for them. There was plain roughness in the language's rawness, and in case the speaker had anger in his tone the last bit of sweetness was also lost.

With passage of time, Alok grew in his height as well the segment underlying beneath his hard-skulled head. Still, those growing years of Alok was physically hectic for Pranati, where her patience and time for her own little space faded away like the haze on the morning glass, which dissolves under even a little bit of warmth.

While Alok was smart enough to defend, and free himself from the clutches of his strict mother's punishment. He was quick to act, intelligent enough to respond, active not at all lazy, still he utilized his qualities to create pain for his mother.

He is still growing, Hari would often utter these words and laugh it off as his wife complained about Alok.

For him, his child never seemed to grow, he was still his little boy, Alok. This quite often bothered Pranati as the child never listened to her, and her husband pretended to be ignorant about all his deeds.

Until the point came, when she stopped sharing his minute details with Hari, complained about his deeds which a mother won't share with someone other than her better half. She took his entire responsibilities upon her own shoulders.

This was true. Alok was tough, but Pranati's punishment was even tougher. She would beat him a few times with a thick cane stick, which felt shockingly harsh to the cold exposed side of his palm.

Still, the cane looked new as it escaped numerous opportunities due to Alok's escaping ways like on the late afternoon of 1983.

Alok was eleven years old, his mother was sitting on the chair, placed close to the open verandah. The winds blew softly, reducing the warmth, which was already lacking in this month of winter. While she was washing the water spinach in the stainless-steel bowl, segmenting into parts of ten to fifteen then chopping it horizontally into pieces. The soft green spinach was growing in abundance within her own pond. So, on weekends while taking bath from this pond, she will swim till the corner which was just meant to preserve the fresh spinach. Then, grab some water spinach floating like lily pads on the surface, break its soft flimsy branches and bring it back to serve it with pieces of prawns merged inside it.

Hari loved the dish of water spinach, minutely chopped with fried potatoes and sliced prawns next to steaming rice.

Lotika, her next-door neighbor expected Alok to be there to be with his mother. Instead, she met Pranati who was aesthetically slicing the potatoes with her boti, a common cooking equipment found in every Bengali household. It has a sharp curved blade like the boat's arch like the ones specifically used to celebrate Onam, fitted on the rectangular wooden stand. So, the woman would keep her right feet on the wooden stand, another on ground, while her fingers would move with swiftness to dice the potato in cubes or scrimps into slices.

'Where is Alok?' Lotika enquired.

Pranati looked puzzled. Lotika started before she even replied, 'Alok climbed on my palm tree, got down like a thief and, then brought down the palm nectar filled earthy brown mud pot along with him. Then, he drank the sweet palm nectar and replaced the palm's sweetness with his own smelly piss. My six years daughter saw him peeing in it. She even threatened him that she would complain to me.

He said, he isn't scared of Lotika, go and tell her everything.'

'Where is this hideous child?' Pranati screamed, waiting for him to respond, so she could search for him with ease. Alok was smart, he would often hide in unknown places during such scenarios. Until, Pranati's anger dissolved into complete pure love, born out of her own fear to lose him. Pranati knew Lotika was filled with anger from the fact that Alok called him by her own name and not adding aunt to it. The ability of not showing respect to someone elder to him was the crime, more than his little misdeeds. Something the land of Sundarbans never forgets to teach the child.

Alok was solving questions of perimeter in his own room, upstairs. The room wasn't enough to fit more than two to three people It was small, still Alok loved it as the thin white-washed wall allowed most of the voices to penetrate, and come inside his room. So, this became his favorite room as his ears, that loved to eavesdrop, listened to the local gossips shared between the women in the open verandah.

He would often hear the small talks between his birth-givers, Baba and Ma, after his Fathers' full day at work come to an end.

The sole thing that his ears couldn't catch were the low mumbles of Grandma. While these gossips like personal stories filled his mind, his left hand moved in a continuous flow. The geometrical figures of squared houses, triangular funnel with dimensions were solved one after another. Today, when he heard the loud, anger filled words of his mother accompanied with little in between talks of Lotika, whose voice was the huskiest on the entire G-Plot.

Within a moment, he ran in speed from the house's back gate, climbed the tree and sat on its innermost branch.

His hiding spots were never fixed. Somedays he would sit on the tall tree covered with huge bushy leaves from the top. Then, other days he would hide behind the cattle-shed or under grandma's bed. While he watched his mother's fierce look and anger filled calls as she searched for him with a cane in her right hand. She would shout out his name, utter rude abusive monosyllables, which sounded more harsher due to lack of urban-sophistication underneath the Sundarbans' language. So, her time, and all of her energy was wasted until her son gave up. While her anger won't last for long, all of this would transform into haunted fear as the pendulum clock moved, crossed every single minute. After all, she feared losing him like her little girl, who was once inside her. He might have drowned in the massive sea, eaten by the waves and became silent forever.

Was he kidnapped?

Pranati always doubted the dark bearded man, who came from Bangladesh to start his own fisher net making business, she was twenty-seven still the worry never faded.

Whenever she would talk about that man, she would always argue with the statement that why couldn't he start his business in his own country.

Hari often said that the roots which create us, also divide us.

'Alok, where are you? Come back to me, my child, I won't beat you.'

After all, this was a mother's heart, for how long she could resist inexistence of the little child from her own eyes. The dusk prevailed owing to the sun's end. Around 4 hours had passed. It was six in the evening.

Still, Alok was nowhere to be seen, not even under Grandma's bed. She was scared, helpless as she searched for him all the while with Lotika, who too left after two hours of trying, tired.

Hari was occupied in his school's administrative tasks, working for a better tomorrow for G-Plot. While Hari's mother had gone to at her sister's place, two blocks to the left of her own home.

She hoped that Alok would reach back home safely before Hari and his mother would come. The fear of losing Alok and getting blamed for all his misdeeds was fastening her already palpitating heart. She was his mother, so it was her responsibility to handle and take care of him. The Sundarbans always blamed the mother for the child's misdeed. Their predominant culture never blamed the father, as if, the child was completely made out of the mother.

The anger in her own tone had melted down into cajoling shouts. Her voice intensified in decibels as she called for him again. Alok could witness his mother's gradual emotional change, still sitting on the top branch of the huge Banyan tree. His work was done and now his mind was ready for action. He purposefully shook the branch and dropped a few leaves on the ground. He was successful as his mother finally noticed him sitting up. She requested him to get down and once he came down, she rushed ahead and hugged him. Alok's heartbeat slowed down as he heard her strong palpitating heartbeat, as if, her heart rate has bounced back into life after the momentary stoppage. But this love was short-lived as soon Alok turned fourteen and finally, his little brother, Alokesh was born.

DISTANT STEAMER

Chapter 5

Pranati was thirteen years younger to Hari. Still, neither she, nor he felt that difference ever coming between them.

When she was about to step into her thirty-first year, she saw herself enlarging as she became pregnant with her second son.

So, with huge responsibilities, sacrifices came chasing up for Alok as his mother's love was now split into two. Plus, unlike him, his little brother was greedy for his mother's affection.

He would always seek for moments to grab her attention.

Will I be wrong, if I said that a child's psychology has been, and will always be selfless and pure? No amount of understanding can get a child to adjust to the situation and not be sad or envious.

Just like an untainted lotus, blooming between the mud but all along brimming with pureness. But the purity does not prevail for long. The negativity gets too much and brings one to a point, making him more real, more human, capable at making errors.

This made Alokesh liable to demand more, have unstoppable hunger of attention. After all he is the little one, not Alok.

Ma, you are my favorite. Baba is always angry, irritated, and scolding me for no reason. Why I can't miss school for few days?

Believe me, Ma, till this day not a single child has hundred percent attendance in my class.

Please, can I stay back at home, won't be repeated tomorrow.

The words evolving out of Alok's mouth coordinated with all his pretentious sad expressions to convince her.

He wished, his mother wouldn't force her this day anymore, tired and exhausted, she would utter those words that Alok's ears were dying to hear, go from tomorrow, you can miss your classes at present.

He knew, if she said yes, it would be a lot easier to convince Baba. As his Baba could be ignorant in almost all matters happening in his little personal space, except academics of his children.

After all, the dreams of middle-class parents are, and will be born out of their child's prosperous future, and in the air of Sundarbans there was nothing prosperous, so Hari just wanted a stable, respectable future for his beloved sons.

Pranati knew and understood the concern of Hari. After all, he was the father, so being scared for his children's fate, left amidst the land of Sundarbans, was normal. Today he was there for him. What will happen when he won't be there?

When he won't be able to stand behind them as their backbone.

So, neither she could disrespect the child's voice, who wasn't grown up enough to know good or bad for himself, nor she wanted to take away the control Hari had on his child. Still, she couldn't deny that Hari was hard on her little boy, forced enough to break down his mental strength.

Go and talk to your Baba, Pranati left the undecided for Hari to decide.

Alok could feel his hopes shattering like chunks of glasses. All this while his mind had lingered a couple of times to the idea of witnessing Inter-island Cricket Tournament, where all his friends were going instead of attending classes on that day at school. The cricket tournament happened once in three months, and Alok has missed the last one due to Baba's strict regulation of classes before happiness. So, he missed all of it; shouting on top of his voice with his friends as the cricket captain of their island shot and the ball crossed the brick fenced wall into a sixer.

After all, this match was between two close islands in South 24 Paraganas of the Sundarbans. One was G-Plot, the place where Hari, and his entire family belonged amidst the crowd of around sixty thousand more natives like them. While the team competing against them belonged to another island, Patharpratima. These two islands were not hundreds of miles apart like the coast of Australia and Indian Peninsula, which wasn't even possible as around eighteen percent of the Sundarbans called West Bengal its home, and the rest was the child of Bangladesh.

So, a stretch of ten kilometers was all that keeps both the islands apart. The locals rode in their local wooden dinghies to trip from one place to another in daylight. There was nothing as fearful as darkness stretching all above Sundarbans.

Don't go to school, I will talk to your Baba, surprisingly Ma gave up to his happiness, he interpreted.

But, this won't be applicable tomorrow, she reminded him in the end.

She had not given up for Alok. It was her little Alokesh's tears that had bothered her. His water-filled eyes were more powerful than Alok's cogent argument. Plus, Alok was pestering her like the buzzling bumble bee circling around the flower without a reason. Alokesh was formed out of Alok's initials, still unlike him his internal construction was vulnerable and insecure. He would start screaming in his non-understandable language with anger as Alok hugged his mother out of love and to convince her for some purpose of his. Alokesh would howl in resistance as if his elder brother has stepped into his marked territorial range.

Sadly, Pranati's love and emotional bonding was no more divided between the two. The other half piece of love, once reserved for Alok, had long travelled from him, and reached the younger one.

After all, her immense love for Alokesh, was cultivated out of his ordinary deeds. Not sublimed within her heart that he was younger than Alok, rather it was the contrasting effect between both of her children.

Unlike Alokesh, his big brother was naughtier, less of a sissy and shared more of him with his Grandma than Pranati. While Alokesh's love for his mother bloomed out of his dependence for his own growth like the dandelions love for Sun. After all, it was her decision to name his little boy, Alokesh, which Hari couldn't disapprove. Alokesh was not confident, strong or naughty, unlike Alok, his shyness, silence and infrequent cries pulled his mother like a strong magnet towards him. Plus, when he was born, she understood what it feels to be a mother. The feeling she couldn't attain due to her being underage when Alok was born.

Pranati interpreted his silence merged with controlled good behavior as his being a well-mannered child. Only later on would she get to know that this wasn't so. That his emotional turbulence was hidden inside his quietness. Who knew all of his present darkness hidden inside his pleasant demeanor would be darker than the cloudy moonless nights of Sundarbans.

After all, generations of psychological teachers have feared all quiet people, whose least sharing minds made them most difficult to predict.

And here, his mother only understood his single emotion, all those times he would break down as six years old like the gushing water breaking down the G-plot's earthwork.

The water flowed from his eyes, nose until Pranati came for his rescue.

While the other side of him would sit with anger ripping inside him as he maintained composure from outside under the wrap of silence. He would pray for revenge and curse them deep down.

After all, he believed that his happiness, all of his soft joys of happiness to be his own true accomplishment, so he shared nothing else, other than his sorrow with his mother.

Whenever, Alok carried Alokesh to the little grocery shop in the market, he would purchase three candies for himself and his little brother. Alok would pop one in his mouth and keep the rest for Baba and Ma.

While Alokesh finished all three in one go, popping the one even before his last one would completely melt inside his mouth. Alok couldn't see the changes in his mother, until he turned sixteen.

After all, love never hides, all of it comes out, becomes visible in other person's eye with age. So, like all of us, he witnessed Pranati's inclination towards him. Still, he never complained, or protested, and gave up as he was older in age to him. After all, his age bounded him to make those little sacrifices from within.

But he didn't know back then that these little sacrifices in life were just like tiny drops of rain in the vast sea. That's how the sea's journey begins.

Alok was fine initially, except for a few days, when his heart could no longer bear the pressure and all of him would spill open, all pain transformed into rage with complacent fear of mixed cacophonous voices. After all, humans have a habit to over-think in their difficult times. He tried to contain it but could never suppress it within himself.

In turn he splurged his heart outside, amidst every one of them to see like his ignorant father, little Alokesh and his own mother, Pranati.

After all, there will be days, when he would slam the wooden door with loud noise, thump his feet with anger steaming inside his head. While he would shout in his shrill adolescent voice. And, piece by piece, all the little bits of love left for the child within Pranati, was gone from her heart like the lilac sky; the one that was never prepared for the dawn

Pranati thought that she had judged Alok with perfection, after all he was the kind of child no mother will ever want to have.

But humans are not perfect, then how can their decisions be?

So was Pranati's decision borne out of her own perception about Alok. The complete lack was in his communication as Alok never communicated the reason, just showed her the rage-filled outcome and Pranati couldn't see what the child went through.

The months of winter had come and gone, Alokesh grew, and meanwhile Alok turned into a complete stranger. Still, this winter as November saw its end, nothing felt different.

While months before winters arrived, autumn and his chilled winds had hit and debarred Halophytic Mangrove forest. After all, G-Plot once upon a time was one among them, all green, Sundari trees next to one another, until human's magic turned all of this into an island.

While Pranati filled drinking water from tubewell, her exposed soft skin close to her elbow could feel the chillness as her mind planned for the homecoming of Kali. After all, the month of November was special in each and every Bengal's household. After the festive departure of Durga, it was the turn of Kali. No big a wonder there considering the Hindus worshipped 34 billion Gods and Goddesses.

Flowered Jasmines fallen on ground produced beautiful fragrance amidst the night air. "Shiuli", was her name, at least that's what the communities from Bengal's origin loved to call.

This time, the same head priest, who last time chanted the mantras of Durga was performing this for Kali, where each para of the mantra came to end with disposition of double red Hibiscus on her feet.

While G-Plot echoed with chains of black Loudspeaker boxes. Meanwhile, his right hand, unoccupied most of the times, would hold the oil wick lamp with five interconnected openings. Circle it in front of the Goddess,

Meanwhile, junior priest poured clarified butter on rashly hand-torn brown coconut husk inside the earthen pot, to set fire and produce smoke all meant for purification.

All of a sudden, the interior of temple was filled with black smoke while the burning rose smelling incense sticks intensified all of this. This ritual of homeness was common inside Kali Temple. Still, unlike other days, the crowd was not in ten or twelve, around three hundred people were standing inside and out of the temple.

While those people under the hope of getting blessed, overlooked the white-painted temple wall, all peeled and blistered as all humans formed chains to circle all around this temple's sphere. While these mid-monsoon suffered walls resembled Ananto like those blisters near his knee formed while catching Prawn in knee submerged Sea water was alike.

'Ma, can I have a tamarind candy?', Alokesh whispered in his mother's ear.

Like each passed year, this time the local fair was arranged on the back side of the temple wall. After all, the Sundarbans had extremely limited activities all around the year to entertain its people in around 1985.

Nothing except few festive fairs decorated with lights all over the market where local goods were available, none exquisite. While local theatre troops performed inside the little habited Sundarbans island all around the festive season. Late mid-night card games all meant for men continued.

Meanwhile, little girls would chase the Pink Candy Man along with little boys of their age. Pink Candy Man had various artificial colored toffees like Cola and Guava flavor, whereas the cola flavored wasn't introduced in the market last season. While he would sit on one stool with his huge, open cloth bag filled-with candies in front of him.

Plus, his collection was remarkable compared to his competitors within neighborhood villages, ranging from orange, Cola-flavored, lime and dried honey, pale-yellow Pineapple, as if, these village children would name the toffee and this man would have it.

Next to him, lingered the smell of Gram-Flour Crisps, deep fried in pure mustard oil attracting more and more mid-aged ladies to her dime store.

Hari was in his white, loose t-shirt and tube-shaping lungi as he stood with eagerness to grab a hot plate of onion fritters, before the cup of his cardamom tea would become tasteless and cold. The school playground with no stage, no marked space, no nothing became the stage for the children.

One local theatre troupe from Kakdwip came down to G-Plot for performing Bon-Bibi's Pala. There were no female characters, all were male, dressed in glimmer and shine, glittering rented clothes, so they could to showcase the female existence. While their own existence; remained unidentified under layers of unaesthetic makeup. Male characters were wearing extra-red rouge on their round cheeks, wigs made from horse hair and layers of foundation to hide their sunburnt freckled skin.

'Ma, how long do we have to wait?'

Bon Bibi's Pala might have started, Alokesh pulled his mother's loose end of the saree as she poured the tea for her mother-in-law inside the cup, until it could fill no more, filled to brim.

We will go in a while, just give me two minutes.

There was no one at home except her, her little child and hot-tempered mother-in-law.

Hari and Alok, had left an hour ago, and now both of them were a part of the crowd who encircled the theatre performance like yellow bumble bees collected for a single purpose. They sat on the grass, laughed out loud and clapped in coordination during an aggressive scene, all the individual voices present becoming one of the crowd.

Rupbaan theatre troupe like all past years, has come this time to G-Plot, performed more for joys of happiness it provided to the crowd, rather than the amount they received in the end.

After all those collected coins were never enough to run a family. For bachelors, yes, without expectations of getting married in near future. Where their home existed, but was devoid of being near complete.

Who would give his daughter to a man known for painting his face, dancing and acting like women?

Inside the bedroom, Pranati was draping her six yards long maroon saree, spun out of pure soft cotton. Saree had a wide border with stories of Bengal; the tales of kings and queens coming home in palanquins, maidens enjoying a leisurely evening and prince chasing the demons on his horse, all carved in perfection with golden colored thread.

Though, pleats of her saree, were messed up, still didn't look unmatched as the background, her own bed tried to imitate her pleats with bunches of over-flowing, disliked sarees, tried blouses and one after another layer of thin petticoat all over the place. As, she loosened the saree to add perfection to her pleats, she saw the reflection of her own rough hands clad in a pair of red, white and round gold bangles as her symbol of married life with Hari.

She gazed longer at how she looked now, in the rectangular mirror of her dressing table. Her own reflection reminded her of the path from the past; the path no longer a part of the present or the future.

Her simple bare eyes were lost, still was this a loss, no. Rather, gain of memories all filled with happiness, the ones bring smile, yet stays afar from present realities.

Pranati felt that she found her past protruding out of glass mirror and touching her mind with reminiscences of loss. After all, those memories of her father, who carried her on his shoulder and brought her the same tamarind candies which Alokesh loved to have.

She was five, when she first time visited the Kali Puja Fair, tightly clasping her father's large thumb with her little fingers. Though, she was bit nervous due to the crowd and fear of losing herself in it. Still, she knew Baba would hold her, not leave for once, until both of them reach home.

When she accompanied him for the second time, all clad in her yellow colored saree with red borders. She was ten years old, and this was the last time she went along with him to witness the festive fair. After all, next time, her feet were dotted with rose colored Alta for marriage as the beautiful, glowing face was approached from the groom's father.

So, she was made to tie knot with an unknown face in the end of December. Still, she could hear those echoes, all of her painful cries as her mother forcibly separated her, made her leave with Hari on the next morning of marriage.

While her mother-in-law strongly clasped her elbow as Pranati all wanted was to run inside the house, her home.

But she couldn't as the heavy pieces of gold and the solid hand of Hari's mother were enough to straddle her back. That night, Hari didn't touch her. Rather he never again tried to feel what it felt like to get inside of her until she turned fourteen. It was Hari, not his mother, who felt nine was too young to bear all of him. He just whispered a few words into her ear amidst the darkness of the room. He said 'we are like two long vertical bamboo sticks constructing ladder out of ourselves, where all those thin horizontal bamboo step-ons need to be juxtaposed. These step-ons were created out of compromises, pleasurable memories, and fights. It won't be always carved out of good memories. Bad times will also hit us. Still, we have to keep moving forward in life, in our relationship and be together.' His words of the daunting night didn't hold much significance to Pranati for many years till she reached the ripe age of nineteen and understood the real meaning behind what her husband had whispered to her ever so often on all those haunting nights when she was scared of him while he was being her only support.

The market was filled with people, some faces she had never seen before, all those who did not belong to this island. Alokesh was holding Pranati's finger, and his big brother was walking on her right side. Hari got tired, so he had already left for home. All of a sudden, the little child's eye glowed with greed hidden inside the iris as his mouth salivated with the thought of guava flavored candies melting inside the warmth of his mouth.

'Ma, look this side, look at those colorful candies', Alokesh narrowed down her eyes towards the small shop while Alok's voice was constantly forcing Pranati to look towards him.

He wanted to show her the new model of the racing car game. Except for the steel tires, the entire body of the car was carved out of wood. Still, Pranati didn't reciprocate to his first child's call, she was busy purchasing candies for Alokesh.

A fire was caught within Alok's heart, which was enough to gather the entire market's attention as he thumped his feet on ground, bringing dust to air. He raised his voice at Pranati like never before while the crowd watched.

Ignorant of her elder son's mental condition Pranati, tired with cacophonies of two colliding noises, decided to calm them both down by giving candies to them. Alokesh was happy. He had got what he had wanted, but Alok threw the candies as far as he could into the crowd. Oblivious, Pranati saved a candy for later.

That night, she distanced the thoughts of neighborhood children's miserable teeth tales, and secretively gave her toffee to the little, her favorite child, Alokesh.

Little did she know that unawares she was distancing Alok from herself, who had gone miles apart from her heart, out of all the left pieces. The sole connection left was that of blood.

Until, the incident happened with the first girl child born out of her. She was special, unlike other lives born amidst the land of Sundarbans, who took birth and departed without notice, she survived.

Pranati called her a complete cry baby, who bore more features of her Baba, Hari, compared to any of her two older brothers. Her face would have given hope to some poet in the west.

After all, she had a brilliant shade of pale yellowish brown with spotted black freckles around the bridge of her nose. Her skin as deep as color of earth was nothing like Hari or Pranati, would have ever wanted.

Hari named her Shyama, the magnificence of darkness. Still, she was laid in Pranati's lap after the birth, her tears were born out of concern for her girl's miserable future.

Who would marry a girl as deep skinned as Earth?

Meanwhile, Hari was promoted as the principle of the single school in the island of G-plot, Vivekananda Vidyamandir. This school never distinguished between girls and boys, the way people belonging from this place did.

So, all responsibilities came down onto Pranati's shoulders. In Hari's absence Alok enacted the role of his own school teacher father like he would knock tight slap on Shyama's over-inflated cheeks in case she dozed off over her open rhyming book. The gravity of his slap was never too hard to hit her, still enough to give her defined undertone of pink blush, awaken her and merge her tears and runny nose like Sundarbans tributaries all down her cheeks.

After all, he wanted to be one of those responsible brothers, his mother would look upon with pride. Unfortunately, his actions never spoke the same language hidden beneath his intentions.

Plus, his mischievous deeds deprived him from all the goodness left that Pranati could have seen within him.

Neither Pranati nor Alok knew, people judged each face with whatever was outside. Character's constructed out of fake intentions, masked gestures, until their true self explodes out of mouth, the relationship and friendship breaking like glass pieces.

These days Pranati's head was burdened with concern arising from Shyama's physical structure as she gained few more kilos with the welcome of late autumn in the last week of October.

Who will marry my Shyama?

Pranati was conversing with Ananto's young, beautiful wife. His wife was fair complexioned, had intense black, hip touching long hair, pointed gourd shaped big eyes, everything a Sundarbans man would love to have in his wife. Pranati would often repeat all of this in her mind.

Still, she would question herself couple of times at least, how did she land up with Ananto?

She often gossiped among her friends in absence of Ananto's wife that Ananto might have casted black magic on her beautiful body, captivated her eyes towards him and bonded it forever into the knot of marriage.

Though, she herself never believed in black magic like Hari, still what was wrong was in spreading some dark rumors.

Alok and Alokesh were playing cricket without a single fielder to support them, Alok as batsman and his little brother as bowler. While her mother-in-law was snoring next to Shyama on bed at this time of dusk, almost twenty past four.

So, Pranati gave responsibilities to Alok before leaving for Ananto's house like to look after little Shyama, take care of Alokesh, still without disturbing grandma's peaceful late afternoon sleep.

While Alok had different plans as he waited for her to step out of the door. He and Alokesh planned to have all the coconut cookies for themselves. He cross-checked the locked door.

Was grandma still sleeping or half-awake?

Alok worked out his mind, until his head came up with an amazing idea, all around hungry for action.

Grandma, I am hungry. Wake up, Grandma,

Alok tried this method a couple of times. Finally, he was assured that Grandma was still asleep as her body seemed like a living corpse, not moving, just the passage of air swelled up her chest and bowed it down. So, her snore was her sole proof of her being alive.

Alok's path was clear as his mother was not at home and Grandma was fast asleep to witness his misdeeds. He tip-toed towards the kitchen hallway as his little brother accompanied him like a dark shady shadow. He held the narrow waist of Alokesh, lifted him upwards to bring down the glass jar filled with coconut cookies, all of it made a few days ago.

This glass jar was Pranati's favorite among all the few glass items she called as her own. The intricate detailed flower protruded with realism through the center of surface, nothing like she has ever seen. While the cookies inside the jar tasted sweet, all made of resins, coconut powder, and pounds of dusted sugar melted under the warmth of his mouth.

All of a sudden, the glass jar slipped from Alokesh's hand as he tried to keep it back to where it belonged. His face was more scared than Alok's face as if his fingers has committed crime, which was serious enough to not expect Pranati's unforgiveness.

Dada, don't tell this to mother?

Alok smiled, this secret will remain between us forever.

While Alok hurried to hand pick the sharp pieces of shattered glass, Alokesh stood in the corner staring at his brother's actions.

While he hand-picked larger chunks, used the broom for the little sharp pieces and the broken crumps of cookies, and in the process he ended up smashing few red ants to death.

Let's go Dada, Ma will be on her way back home. Finally, Alok felt that the mother's love, which separated them, also bound them in times of need.

Shyama's sleep was complete, and her old grandma was still snoring beside her. So, four and a half years old Shyama left her bed, came downstairs to search for her two elder brothers.

Her search wasn't completely futile as the broken cookies jar still had few left pieces inside it. She was excited while all the language of greed for cookies was written in her eyes.

Something her mother won't have given to her overweight daughter. Here, more than being overweight the addition of her being a daughter caused her more pain.

After all, Pranati was conscious about her physical unattractiveness, and her approaching marital age maximum ten years down the lane. She herself was married at an age of nine, knew how painful it would be to send her daughter to someone else's house at such a young age. Still, it would be better than getting abandoned within the community for keeping herself at home.

Don't give this little girl fried potatoes or crisps, how will I find a decent groom for her?

She is already overweight and dark, no one is going to give his son by looking at you, Pranati would often raise her voice against Hari for spoiling the girl's habit. While, this time in absence of her brothers and mother, she could reach for her unaccustomed jar of sweetness. So, to grab them all within her small fist in one go, she moved with speed and few sharp pieces pierced her feet. She screamed with fear as drops of blood fell on the floor.

Though, there were no bloody scratches or deep cuts, but all of this was big enough for a little child, who hasn't seen blood before. Grandma came rushing towards the open kitchen aisle. She cleaned the wound, applied ointment balm even on the places where there were no cuts and her tricked worked. Finally, the little girl gave a toothy smile to her grandma and slept back on her comforting bed hugging her.

Though Pranati had always been hot headed, but nothing boiled her blood more than this entire incident that took place that afternoon. She was sure, this was another mischief of Alok.

Before night as the sun dusked with its own end, she trashed Alok like an unknown thief. While his little brother heard slashes of his father's belt slapping with roughness on his brother's back.

He heard his older brother's ear piercing screams, begging for leaving him this time. He also promised that he won't repeat it again. Still, Alokesh couldn't didn't have the guts to confess that it was his mistake.

This was the last time, Pranati decided to bother about Alok's future. For her, Alok was further away from her than Hari was. Ultimately, the crack was formed.

The scar of that evening always remained with Alok. Whenever, he planned to steal mangoes or cookies, the broken face of Shyama as he returned back home flashed like a reflection from the past. His mind retained the image. Still, the foolish girl showed her cuts to Alokesh, as if, he wasn't her deserving brother. Rather, not the one deserved to be known after being responsible for her such condition. Still, the secret of Alokesh's fault never found an open window to escape and reach Pranati's ear. After all, his competition wasn't his little brother, just a little space inside his mother's heart.

Six years passed in between like the granular sand changing its surrounding from upper glass bulb to lower, turn, and again upper glass bulb to lower, all stifled within an hourglass.

Alok changed as his educational pressure increased with each new forward mark after passing the last exam. So, his mischievous activities couldn't find an outlet, submerged and finally drowned under the burden of people's expectation from him. Especially, Hari's expectation from his eldest son, who would support the family in his absence, run the kitchen supplies and hold them together like the flower whose beauty exists in keeping the petals, leaf and stem attached. So, Hari spared out time on weekends to cross-check all the numerical solved by his grown-up child, Alok. His father cared for him that's what Alok believed, until one silly mistake in calculation caught Hari's eye. Then, Alok felt his words piercing his skin, deep and hurting the places it shouldn't be.

You wish to abandon your land, become like these men who have taken everything from G-plot, yet given nothing in return.

Hari would personally mention the person's name, who failed in one grade, next year became a dropout, then feed himself on father's wealth until it perished. Hari wanted him to take the advantage of education, become a doctor, after all this was their sole means of support to overcome the barriers pertaining inside a lower-middle class household. Still, he never wished him to cross the island for livelihood, sustain his profession on an unknown land and serve the unknown faces, as if, all his hard work and crossing the channel, was meant just for the educational degrees not available amidst the small island of G-plot.

Here, students drop-out from school within months of joining because either there are no good teachers or the ones good at it are lesser in number. 'Being a teacher and a father, I would reach out to you, help you in all possible means, still all my efforts went in vain', Hari added. While Alok listened to most of the words, his head was hung with more acts of shame, than the feeling of it.

Finally, around 1989, Alok passed with second division in his twelfth board exams. To Hari and him, this was the final directional call towards making into one good college in the town, Kolkata.

Something, G-plot still couldn't afford to build for his own children. So, with the final call, it was time for Alok's departure.

Hari has already touched his mid-forties with the end of last month. Though most of the time, his white hair were lost within his black strands, until the swift move of salty wild air caressed it with love, as if, his grey hair played peekaboo amidst the patches of black ones.

Today, he was sitting next to Pranati, wherein between small talks, his wife packed, "Narkel Narru", concoction of heated coconut powder and jaggery syrup made into round balls under the soft pressure of palm.

In Case, her dessert looked distorted, she would dip her hand till wrist in water and with lightly wet palm she would break the soft, warm "Narkel Narru" to create perfection in its external shape. This was one of those tricks, she had learned from her mother-in-law as she stepped into making the desert first time two decades ago. While she gave final touch with one piece of dried grape on top of all the rounded balls. Side-by-side, she stuffed them inside the tin container. While, all along Hari stared at her pale and confused face.

Your little son isn't going for forever. After all, he would only be coming back once he completes his education.

Pranati nodded.

You should be proud Pranati, he will come back and serve all of us. He would become a good teacher just like me, Hari added to console her.

'Pranati, you just wait for the month of autumn. He will come back, lie on that bed near the verandah and demand you to make his favorite spicy crab curry throughout his entire vacation.'

'He loves to have it with steamed white rice and freshly diced shallot.' Pranati had a corner smile on her face as she finally said these words to Hari.

Hari was successful, as he brought back the lost smile on her face. But she just had it for a while until she lost it again amidst the oblivion.

Though, he himself was consoling her, still deep inside he was broken from the waves of parting. After all, Alok was, and has always been his beloved child.

He was Alok, his first essence, who brought the pain of inexperienced fatherhood.

Still, all of this pain had its own share of joy, suppressed amidst layers of happiness as Alok was about to fulfil one of his own dreams.

While Pranati's pain evolved out of her own imaginative ignorance like a kind of tension born from different, unfelt, feel of pain.

So, this pain, which dissected her heart from past few weeks, made her numb and then all of a sudden her beautiful smiles coming on the face, somehow vanished.

All along, she imagined the pain of losing her little son, Alokesh just like her older one, Alok.

Though, she wasn't excited about Alok's departure as she was his mother. Still, all those moments, she imagined Alokesh departing for higher studies just like Alok, and her mind gloomed with an unknown shadow of sadness.

Inside the bedroom, after crossing the open aisle, there was grandma, who was neatly folding a bunch of clothes as Alok standing next to her, stuffed them all inside the tin trunk.

He thought about Kolkata under the verge of fascination inside his head. Couple of times before, he has gone to Kolkata, but all were for brief period of time.

All those last times, he had travelled to Kolkata with Baba, almost an entire day took him to reach his favorite spot, Victoria Memorial. He was hardly fourteen that year but his mind like all human minds memorized each and every minute details of happiness as if, those stories weren't older than a few weeks.

'Baba, when will you take me to Kolkata? You promised me last month.'

'Alok, my good boy, I will definitely take you next month after I have corrected the exam papers of class eighth graders.

Aren't you my good child, won't you understand Baba's problem?'

'Baba, summer has gone, autumn has also ended, and look winter is in its peak to approach. Now, if we don't go, not this time, when we will go?' Reflection of inflexible attitude in his demands was visible to his Baba.

'Why didn't you take me last time? You said we, you and I, will go together. Then, you left while I was still attending my English class in school.'

To change his topic, just like any other normal parent, Hari picked up a casual topic of conversation. He asked, 'Have you completed your homework?'

'I will do it in a while,' said a disheartened Alok.

'Listen, wait till your winter break, it's just near the corner.'

'You, your little brother, your mother and I, all of us will go together.' That winter they did go to Kolkata, but not all of them. Just he and his Baba as Alokesh won't leave his mother's side and Pranati had responsibilities of home like that of taking care of her mother-in-law.

So, at sharp five under a not so clear morning, even before the sun dawned out its way to spread brightness in G-plot, Hari and Alok came near the offshore to ride on a boat.

The boat wasn't huge, rather a small dinghy with some food supplies stored at its back, to serve brunch and late afternoon meal to passengers. Three boatmen rowed the wooden dinghy, and not more than six local natives along with them occupied the space inside. Around fifteen minutes past five, boatmen rowed his small boat away from this shore to reach another shoreline. Finally they reached and rested near the offshore of Kakdwip around the same time as dusk.

Like the concoction of two words, milk and honey, this land mass was given the name of Kakdwip, where "Kak" meant crow and "Dwip" signified an island. In short, island filled with crows.

But Kakdwip was neither brimming with crows, nor this was an island. Rather, all of this, was a place stuck within the map of West Bengal as a whole, not like her distant cousins, small inhabited islands in Sundarbans, who are separated from the mainland as dots amidst the vast waters of the Bay of Bengal.

And, to reach Sealdah from Kakdwip, passengers boarded a local train, all of which occupied another five hours of their life in one go. So, Hari and his little son, rode on the local train and reached Sealdah, the major passenger and goods train hub of Kolkata.

Till the time, both of them, entered a cheap government guesthouse near Garhia, the sun was on its route to dawn again. The outside was bright with streetlights, lights peeping through the windows of huge palace like buildings at the Park street of Kolkata.

Though, Alok would often wish to witness this entire scenario throughout the year, all three hundred and sixty-five days, but this just remained his wish, the one that never was fulfilled. We often do not register such minor details of life in the noises thrown at us from the city but people like Alok crave for those things in life which are not a part of you.

Next afternoon, as the father and his son visited the Victoria Memorial, a booklet of famous tourist spots caught Alok's attention. To him, it resembled more like one geographical magazine, where one-liner details were under all those pictures.

Alok flipped along those pages as his big round eyes monotonously moved like a pendulum, as if, someone was pulling the thin rope to his circular eyeballs. While Hari adjusted his oval rimmed power glasses with his left hand, cause his right hand was holding the scalding tea poured inside the little bowl-shaped mud tea cup. His posture was leisurely as always as he was sitting on the high wooden stool near the roadside Tea Stall while his legs hanged, more often than not not touching the ground.

Baba, see here, Alok pointed towards the picture of a Royal Bengal Tiger.

The location seemed to be somewhere near Gosaba, the author had even mentioned, and described its beautiful geo-politics in a few lines below the picture. While the backdrop inside the picturesque picture was of green, mysterious Sundarbans forest. Nothing unusual or with any sharpness of newness, no signs of autumn, no existence of harsh cyclonic winds, nor yellowing of any leaves.

All the same, just the same. While the tiger was jumping out of the forest to swim inside the narrow water tunnel, an incomplete jump as the tiger's feet were still in air. Though, the image looked fierce, still the jump of the tiger felt like it was thrown out of the forest as if it no longer owned that land.

Alok with pure intention, read out those words aloud. So that his father could also listen and understand the dilemma going through his head.

"Sundarbans is the largest mangrove forest in the world."

While speaking, Alok could imagine those images like little snapshots rushing towards his mind, one after the other.

The little red Hermit Crabs or Mud creeper, a kind of fish who would leave water, still survive outside water in mud. While he could feel how unique his roots were in this world of billions. Still, he and his communities never bothered to think about it.

'Why Gosaba was reflecting the entire Sundarbans?

They haven't mentioned about us.

What about the Southern part of the Sundarbans?

Neither is Sundarbans all about forest. Isn't it Baba?'

Hari's mouth burned with pain as strokes of Alok's questions intruded his peaceful sip of hot milk tea in the late afternoon.

Though, he took a few harsh deep breaths as he constructed those answers inside his mind. Still, he couldn't give structure to his thoughts as all he wanted was to better explanation to Alok.

Hari slid his fingers to grab the booklet from him.

As, he started reading couple of initial lines about Shanti Niketan on the first page, all together, his eyes moved towards the bottom of the page.

"Around fifty-two islands are inhabited, then came one small description about Gosaba"

All this time Alok was smiling at him like an idiot.

As if, he was satisfied with the given description.

Still, he was Hari, his father, who knew what he wanted to know about them, nothing more or less, all about their existence.

Unfortunately, in this round world, there existential stories were unknown. Even, the world map, which showed them as little islands amidst the dark Sundarbans didn't know that all those little islands had different historical stories, just like there little shapes, their composition and culture, all were different.

When Lord Curzon visited the Sundarbans, he named almost all the islands in the Southern Sundarbans based upon its aerial shape like G-Plot was named because of its G-shaped structure. Then, the island next to it, I-Plot, cause its outline was that of the alphabet I. All of these islands' beauty lied amidst their differences. After all, among all those deforested forests transformed into islands, Alok and Hari's little stories resided in one among them, known as G-plot.

Length of G-plot wasn't more than fifteen kilometers, while this beautiful island's breadth couldn't cross three kilometers. Around thirty to thirty-five thousand people lived on this island they called Bura Burir Tat, the oldest still the farthest one from mainland, Kolkata till the East India Company explored this beautiful place and renamed it to G-Plot.

Though, diverse products in agricultural fields bloomed all around the season, still amidst all of these bamboos were sure to find themselves a place. While fisheries like large black striped prawns, lobsters, red hermit crabs, and hundred to two hundred varieties of other small and big fishes, all existed with each other in peace and love.

Though, G-Plot was whole and complete, still, all of this was divided into segments for better understanding of area-wise crop production and landowner system back in the mid 1980s.

Uttar Sundarganj was one part, where Alok and his father, Hari resided.

This location if translated from soothing Bengali Syllables to English would mean Beautiful North, where

"Uttar" signified North while "Sunderganj" meant beautiful land mass.

Plus, the word, North, even justifies its position within the entire map of G-Plot.

While Dakshin Sunderganj, Paschim Sunderganj and Sitarampur were rest of the divided proportions on this island.

Everything begins with a hope born out of dream, so did Alok's grandfather's desire to build one school for his inland children.

During mid 1940s, Alok's grandfather, pretty much in his young days founded this school for the locals in G-Plot. He was a fisherman, though he himself never got an opportunity to come out of the stigma of his own profession, nor could he literate himself to come out, and seek for new life but, Hari, his child, the one made out of half of him, was able to do so. After all, he was the first graduate from Kolkata within the entire G-Plot. Though, each year, one after another student, left for Kolkata, to pursue multiple degrees and bring home first division but Hari's Baba could feel his heavier heart as all the proudness for him lied there. After all, Hari, his son was the first one to do so, and he was right that the supreme feeling of first never fades.

So, as promised, Hari came back to his own G-Plot after getting his degree and took the role of teaching Physics to Eleventh Graders at school.

All his colleagues, teaching in the local school, were mere High School Pass, a criterion enough to just teach till class twelfth, Alok was definitely someone who stood out. It wasn't that he hadn't got offers to teach in Semi-Urban regions of Kolkata after leaving Calcutta University with a degree in Physics but Hari knew, sun would change into moon, moon would become sun, still his son's promise given to his Baba won't change dimensions. It will remain the same.

"Your heart is like that bud, all along waiting to bloom, so more this flower grows, more it contributes to this beautiful world. Still, always remember to never detach from your roots, your own home." His Baba's words bounded his feet. He knew he could never wander too far, and for the growth of a few more, he suffocated his own dreams and stopped achieving unaccustomed heights.

He returned to his home. Nothing had changed, other than calling his state free from the hands of British Colonizes, and singing national anthem on India's Independence. G-Plot was now under the rule of village Panchayat, where assembly of five local members judged their faith with little pieces of biasness hidden inside their hearts. It still had to wait for the basic amenities like electrical connections, a hospital to deliver a fetus out of a mother's womb, better educational facilities like colleges or universities were a far cry.

Once a week, a medical superintendent would come down from Kolkata to serve the natives of G-Plot, all inside his single roomed chamber next to the spread of local evening market.

Plus, the narrow roads aligning to embankment, weren't broad, so this road could only transport bicycles all along its route.

Still, the sole meaningful creation of G-Plot was this High School; quite a tall building with a huge open football ground in front, standing without further possibilities like the stagnant green caterpillar, who could neither hide inside the cocoon nor evolve as a colorful butterfly. Still, their educational barrier couldn't cease their income for livelihood as their mainstream profession was neither to be a doctor nor engineer. Rather, the jobs which city-dwellers called errant like owning and running a small grocery shop on the main market, and knitting fish nets with lightweight plastics to catch prawns and selling them in Kolkata was what these students were aiming at. Sons as teachers in the houses of G-Plot would happen once in a blue moon, so Hari's Baba was blessed with luck there.

"Fish is like gambling. What will you catch next depends upon your luck, whether huge or small. Here, you are an instrument in the vast sea with nowhere to go, so just wait with patience until your luck returns back." Hari's Baba would often share lessons of life with him.

Finally, Hari gathered patches of unfragmented thoughts, and started.

"Our history is as old as other well-known places in India but it will take time for better recognition."

Alok smiled as if he got the satisfactory answer he wished to hear from his Baba. The dots were clear like when the priest said that the sculpture of Shiva was found out and while digging out the loose black alluvial soil from around it the shovel had hit the top of the 'shivling' and chipped the head a little. Nevertheless, it was extracted from under the buries of the dark soil and was worshipped as the ultimate God till the end of G-Plot saw itself.

A temple was constructed, all around, to create Shiva's home, where the faith of his followers resided.

How do they know then how old is their history?

How the Shiva's sculpture came out from meters of deep digging beneath the brown-earth surface? Meanwhile another incident, few months before came to Alok's mind as if his own mind was popping snapshot of images, beautiful ones to prove that Baba was right, G-Plot isn't the new born child of Sundarbans created by the father of winds and mother water. This was weaved for lives centuries ago, found by people, they resided, made their kingdom, still couldn't stay forever.

Often sudden arrivals of anger-filled water drowned everything inside it. But there is a beginning to every end, so even G-Plot saw its rebirth. All from scratch as new green Sundarbans forest evolved, followed up with abandoned children of this universe, who were hit by their own faith so they left for the mainland.

He and Ananto's elder son, Asim were hand-picking little pebbles, which varied in different color ranges like complete black, few off-white with tiny patches of dusty yellow and shallow green.

But none of these tiny pebbles were to be kept with Asim or Alok. They were to be thrown back into those deep waters.

When both of them had nothing much to do, they would stand in ankle-deep water and compete against each other that whose pebble reached the farthest spot.

Meanwhile, a half broken golden coin caught Alok's attention. This coin was around 3 cm in length and breadth. The coin's diameter was turned to radius, because of its lost half.

Alok picked up the glistening piece, all in glory under the beams of sun. Those little carved words encrypted on the coins, made no sense to both of them. But like a piece of treasure Alok kept it inside his pocket. Asim could have argued about who would keep the gold but he didn't because fairly, Alok had found it and he was the rightful owner of the little piece of value. Plus, he knew that little Alok was an adamant lad. His confrontation would have costed him their friendship of eleven years. Later in the evening, when Alok showed it to his mother she thought that the coin was just gold-plated as who will hide or leave such a huge and weighty piece of gold near the shoreline?

Until, she took it to the person whose eyes knew its value, G-Plot's own local goldsmith,

'This is a pure gold coin. Where did you hide your adverse possession for so long?'

The goldsmith under his crooked smile reflected humor in his tone, something Pranati didn't like. She avoided answering him. Next morning, the gold coin with years full of unknown history was weighed and melted down to form a necklace, traditional long bell earring, and a peacock designed Saree belt, all for her little daughter, Shyama's marriage. She conceived only one desire, to get her settled down. Even if the world of marriage couldn't see her beautiful face in her brown skin, they might see all this amount of jewels and money attached to her. After all, Pranati was her mother.

Her right or wrong was unjustifiable under the validation of her own society and her society only wished for her daughter's marriage. All even before Shyama could decide wrong and right for herself.

CITY OF HAPPINESS

Chapter 6

Kolkata wasn't his home.

Still, all those times, he knew as he explored this city of happiness that there was something special about Kolkata. And, this feeling for Kolkata never saw its own end. He found some newness in all of his fresh visits.

Like the hustle bustle of unknown lanes, yellow painted taxis chasing time, or those narrow lanes aligning like parallel lines to the streets of Jadavpur, Kolkata always presented something new to Alok.

While these streets were a sea of human under whose shadow lied some happy people, some sad faces, still each and every unknown face just seemed to move back and forth like non-uniform waves of sea in Sundarbans.

Alok's nostrils could feel the difference. The air he inhaled was nothing like G-Plot. It just smelt of polluted charcoal. While those old buildings across "New Market" looked promising as its construction was still going strong even after a few centuries. Sometimes these faded parts of history only needed few retouches of paint to feel the new. So, that's what those locals did like changing the rust infested iron window, then painting them with popping out shades of red.

Still, this city had its own stories of survival.

1On days of visit, he and his Baba, had nothing specific to do, both of them, would catch a tram, reach Victoria Memorial and sit down on the dry lawn to feast on Jhal Muri. This was one of his favorite mixture, made out of puffed rice mixed with spices and a tablespoon of raw mustard oil, which was purchased from the local stall outside the Victoria Memorial's main gate.

Hari loved Victoria Memorial but this wasn't Alok's favorite spot. Rather, it was the one next to this—the white colored building of the Indian Museum near Jawaharlal Nehru Road.

So, tightly holding on to Hari's little finger, he would often revisit this museum, and go through the lines of antic items, all secured inside the locked transparent glass. Though, he loved almost all those sections, still that Bronze Gallery inside the Archaeological Section was of his personal favorite, where the South Asian Sculptures had stories to tell like his Goddess Manasa back at home.

There were little description under the wrap of summaries that were written on steel plates, pasted on the lower corner of the glass frame for all to read.

All were stories, still the sole difference lied in their birth as all those beautiful stories came from far east.

Alok was anxious as packed his luggage with his grandma. He has never completely departed from his Sundarbans root, where returning back home depended upon his own unknown fate. Plus, his mind wasn't at peace as he kept self-doubting if he will ever be able to cope up within such an urban atmosphere away from baba, grandma, Alokesh and his adolescent lover, whom he had met only a year ago.

All away, far from his belongings, chasing something yet not knowing what will be bestowed. All the while, the date on the calendar showed June of 1990.

'Did you keep your pair of sweaters? The one, I had spun last summer?' asked his worrying grandma.

'Yes, Grandma.'

Alok was done with his packing. Finally, his another milestone of stories within his journey of life was about to begin.

Though, he had wanted to take up Mathematics as his Major subject, he couldn't as English pulled down his score in the final report card. So, his own realities inflated his dreams of expectation.

Was it Alok's fault? Not really. An infested root can never bloom fresh beautiful flowers.

After all, G-Plot had always faced an issue of proper, qualified English teacher in the local school.

Plus, for a child coming from a Bengali Medium School from an isolated rural island, this was enough. So, for the very first time, he felt jealous of all those good scoring Kolkata Boys, who were not deprived of little needs, dreams and desires in life. All he could feel was ambitions cursed because of his birth amidst the Sundarbans, which shook him out of dreams, and ambitions changed his grounds of prosperous life. So, he finally got admission in Chittaranjan College of Commerce in Calcutta University under the course for Bachelors of Commerce.

'Baba, I will come back during my autumn break.' Alok said.

Though, his masculine voice shook a bit as he witnessed Baba's forcible smile on his pale lips.

Those lips spoke million words, enough to break him down from inside. His Baba, was standing next to his mother on the road aligned to the embankment. While Pranati was holding his little brother's hand in a tight grip as the child too was angularly clinging on to her.

His second little sister, Supriya, the one born after five years of Shyama's birth played with loose soil. A couple of times rubbing it against her dress to clean her hands. She was creating her own world out of her own four years of experience. Alok settled down, adjusted his tin trunk within the small space near the lower corner deck of the boat. The boatmen started rowing his wooden paddle back and forth in the sluggish mud colored water. While he stood still and stared at Baba, and G-Plot for the better view. It felt like his last time.

Finally, the boat swiftly moved away from G-Plot through the narrow streams, lined with dense halophytic mangrove forests along both the sides. While the intertwined roots of Sundari trees, which were exposed above the riverine created shadows at this dawn.

See there, the lean boatman was pointing towards the right side of the bank as their boat moved towards Bhagwatpur. After all, Bhagwatpur, was known for its incredible varieties and numbers of crocodile. Meanwhile, the forest along both the sides was still going strong.

Crocodile, Alok said without much interest. Even, boatman realized his disinterest.

Why was he showing crocodile to me?

Sundarbans had seen enough crocodiles from a distance numerous times like when they crossed the narrow silent streams before reaching the mouth of the Bay of Bengal, heads of crocodile would afloat on water, few would be seen sun basking.

Next time, when he pointed out to him, Alok understood his point.

One sun glazed crocodile was lying on the muddy bank as the sunbeams basked his textured skin. All along, a slimy mud creeper jumped from one corner of his huge, long tail to another.

As if, this mud creeper found a game to pass his time and the crocodile, uncared and unbothered, was fast under the wrap of his sleep. This entire scene produced a curved grin on his face. But it couldn't sustain longer as the remorse hit him. He was already missing baba. This beautiful place of Sundarbans was soon going to become a part of his memory. And, all these memories would wind its cord again and again during his low feeling days in Kolkata.

All of a sudden, the narrow streams amidst the Tiger Land changed into wider openings. Here, the change was quite abrupt so the boat started struggling, jerking up and down. The boatman was calm, so was Alok. Finally, after an hour of struggle, the boat landed into the silent, quiet stream.

Fireflies started hovering over the boat as darkness started spreading with the end of day. After almost eight hours of ride, Alok reached his destination. Though, it was far from the town of happiness, illuminated Kolkata was still far better off than the place he came from. This was a small village road with much better off roads, where basic necessities of peaceful lives were available and the locals did not fear the arrival of frequent cyclones.

Still, their population was a one-third of G-Plot, where most of the people were involved in mainstream professions and dealt with exporting fisheries coming from the little fifty-four islands. Just like all his previous visits with baba, this time also he stopped near the sweet corner. His eyes rolled over the displayed sweets on the other side of the glass.

The large bellied owner moved his newspaper around the deserts to get rid of the hideous flies but they kept returning. The expression on this man's face was neither welcoming nor discomforting. The entire shop was much like a big hall with a partition in the middle so that the incomplete sweets were on the other side of the partition. Alok was sitting next to a middle-aged man, who looked like a local, pretty much busy in reading the newspaper and taking infrequent sips of his hot milk tea.

A young boy in his dusty khaki half pant came to take his order.

'One malai chomchom and a cardamom tea.' He knew what he wanted so even as the little boy offered him the menu card he placed his order.

Malai chochom was his personal favorite desert, a simple elongated desert made out of sponge like dumpling with cheese curd and semolina dough, then dipped in sugar syrup, all chilled and layered on with fat cream.

'When will the next train to Sealdah arrive?'

'Around twenty-five past five.' he got the reply.

This sweet shop, a resting place for most of the locals travelling between Namkhana to Sealdah, was quite a popular one.

Time charts of the local trains, were pasted on the wall, next to the fridge, which never changed except on days the rain God poured his sweetness on Earth. Until, each and every train travelling on that route delayed including the humans.

Finally, he paid the price of his evening snacks as the shopkeeper counted the coins he got and went back to flying away the flies and insects from the deserts.

Alok was tired when he boarded the train. And not a single seat was vacant. There was no space to breathe or move his legs. This train was heavily crowded, where those local vendors were hanging near the door to get down or ride on to it fast. Among them, few were selling sliced up Guavas with sprinkled black salt, and one man carried a white Polystyrene cartridge stuffed with large chunks of ice and cold drink bottles inside it as he shouted, 'Pepsi, Miranda'.

Some were also selling some inexpensive artificial jewelries and the multi-purpose ointment balm, Tiger Balm; the one most popular in the Southern West Bengal. Finally, Alok got a seat as a woman got down in Jadavpur. On days, when he had come with baba, he would be happier to sit next to the large open window of the train, where the wrought iron window rods looked like those Spanish well covers, but not so much this day.

Under the iron rod's uncomfortable support, he rested his head as he dozed off in a while after staring at the constant sight of darkness outside and the flickering yellow bulbs inside.

'The train will go in the depot.' He was startled as he heard the deafening loud voice of the train guard, who was trying to wake him up as he shook his body with all force left within him.

In a moment of rush, he even forgot to speak those five letters, "sorry" and got down at Sealdah and took a reverse train till Dhakuria. Then, walked for another fifteen minutes until the placard outside the two-floored building caught his attention. This placard didn't seem to be taken much care as the initials of the mess name were missing.

'BOKA Mess', he read it aloud.

After an entire day's exertion and sadistic thoughts, this mistaken, little detail bought grin on his face. This word, Boka, meant an idiot in Bengali. Still, none of this seemed to bother him, nor did he care about his new address, till the time, money escaping out of his pocket was lesser than he had expected.

The best thing that worked in his favor was that the owner would not be intimidated of his doings as he was residing a few kilometres away from the Mess. So, he felt relieved as his mistakes won't be recorded and messaged back to baba. The room given to him, was nothing like the one he had left behind. The turquoise colored paint on the interior walls of his room was something new. It was just enough for a single person with one single folding bed, small table and a wooden wardrobe. All the rooms weren't same, some were a few feet larger while some just had enough ventilation. Alok's room came under the second category. Still, he was excited with his new-found freedom and the start of his new life. Enthusiastically, he arranged a few pairs of striped shirts, some faded t-shirts, some shorts and a tailor stitched grey pant in the cupboard.

Still, something was missing as the open wardrobe with hunger-filled eyes looked at him as an addictive dysfunction, demanding him to fill more of it. But this was all he had.

'Are you new here?' Boys from the neighboring rooms came to know him and soon filled his room with gossips.

But he felt disconnected as the language he spoke though Bengali, didn't have an urbane touch of sophistication like them, all rustic with sounds of roughness.

Their conversation revolved around new authors, football matches and blockbuster Tollywood movies. All of them, even fantasized about the reel chemistry of Uttam Kumar and Suchitra Sen. Alok lied to not fall out of space.

After all, G-Plot neither had electric connection nor television sets, and till then Alok had hardly watched two or three movies, which were neither romantic nor interesting for adolescent eyes. But none of them could sense his beautifully weaved lies, which Pranati would have caught in minutes.

Alok couldn't clearly remember the date, the year was 1984, a regular Saturday evening. When Asim, Ananto's son broke down the news of football match that he had planned to witness.

'Are you going all by yourself? Where is this happening?'

Asim nodded his head to his first question, and added 'Patharpratima' to the next.

This beautiful word, Patharpratima signified sculpture carved out of stone. This too was an island, similar to G-Plot in numerous aspects, but bigger in terms of regional area. Both these islands weren't far off from each other. To and fro distance between the islands could be covered in a total of four hours, which included travelling from G-Plot to Patharpratima, and then back to G-Plot.

None of them were old enough to presume the travel without baba or their mother's permission. Asim was hardly in tenth grade and Alok was two years younger to him. Plus, he knew that Pranati would never give him the permission nor take him along with her as she herself was submerged in her home related responsibilities.

So, he and his close friend, Asim, both paid the boatman a few coins which they had saved out of their previous month's pocket money, and left without informing anyone.

While the football match knitted memories for an entire lifetime as his favorite team kept on hitting the ball towards the goalpost. Everything was routing as per his plan of action, until the vault of heaven changed its color into wild dark blue, and started downpouring with tremendous enthusiasm.

Alok was confused, scared, what if mother finds out where his son was? Plus, none of the boatmen were accepting even double the amount to ride across the anger fudged waters.

Finally, without any option he decided to ask for shelter in a random local shop. One shopkeeper couldn't decline the request as they were little children. Next morning as the sunbeams unfolded, he and his own, Asim rode on the boat to return back to their home, G-Plot.

Till then, almost half of the G-Plot knew that these little, mischievous boys were missing as their little world lived and survived their hard times through sole piece of entertainment, gossips. As their boat was reaching towards the riverine, Asim saw Ananto, all drenched and tired still sitting on his anchored fishing boat as if he hadn't slept. All the while he was just waiting for his son, only him.

As soon as, Ananto and his son exchanged glances, he rushed towards his approaching boat. His knees were half submerged under deep muddy mush waiting for his son to get down the boat and enter G-Plot. Still, his welcoming wasn't something unexpected as unlike Hari, Ananto carried more emotions, and less rationale within himself. One slap, another slap, where the last one was always harder than the last one. Still, he didn't touch Alok.

How could he after all he didn't bore his own blood?

So, he held Alok's hand and dragged him with all his power to lead him towards his home.

While Pranati after shedding tears the entire last night, was worn out and for the first time she didn't beat him. Though, numerous times after this incident, he planned to watch cinema in Kakdwip's local cinema hall, yet, neither Asim nor he himself ever got the guts to do so.

Meanwhile, his new-found friends within this mess left him, to meet another new student, who had also arrived the same evening. He thought about how the first day is going to be at college tomorrow, the circle of butterflies within his stomach gave him anxieties. Still, all those anxieties weren't as uncomfortable as eavesdropping to the talk of those boys, who mixed and became one among the crowd. These boys didn't belong to influential, rich families as no parent without the tension of few extra bucks would ever send his child to mess, not this one. Still, their upbringing was within average middle-class families of Kakdwip or had found home in houses next to narrows lanes of South Barasat. In simple words, their conditions were better off than his, and he was self-conscious about their opinion regarding him.

Tomorrow there will be a new dawn, that's all he thought before falling asleep.

HE AND SHE

Chapter 7

Hasn't he left for Kolkata?

Her female classmates giggled as those words came out of their mouth. Snehalata heard the one, who uttered those words, even knew who she was. Still, she decided to remain mum.

Though, this entire scenario wouldn't have been same, if her Alok, would have just visited Kolkata for a shorter duration.

She might have reciprocated her lines with an imperceptible pinkish blush on cheeks. While along the line of blush, she would have shown her big eyes, all black kohl adorned to play along with her lines of teasing, not at all to warn her.

While to her, this day felt different, as if, an immense fabrication of remorse and pretension to show happiness has hit her, then shattered them all into pieces.

After all, she couldn't decide, which one to feel altogether. She should be filled with soft joys of happiness for Alok as he achieved partial amount of his dreams that he lured for or she should for her loss, her wilt, where in his utter space of accomplishment all of her was left behind, alone with those memories that they both cherished together.

Should I write him a letter?

She asked her close friend, Aparna, who was sitting just few inches next to her. Both of them together on the same caramel painted wooden bench.

The bench was next to the small, open window on the right-hand side. While their class was supposed to start fifteen minutes before, yet, as always, their English teacher was late.

Still, the black board was filled from words of the last biology class. Here, the outline of dissected flower's physical structure was beautifully described. Plus, the world 'Mallika', which meant Jasmine in English was also written. The children of Sundarbans lcarnt everything in their own comfortable linguistic language, which wasn't possible, if that Mallika became jasmine, all in English Literature.

Aparna dropped her curried potato within the lower segment of her steel box, then picked it up again with her fork. She was startled with the amount of guts residing within Snehalata.

'Have you even thought?'

'Of what?'

'What if you get caught?'

Aparna's blatant voice was loud enough to reach those boys sitting on two benches next to them. So, one of them twisted around, and gave her one eyebrow raise. As if, these girls were pronouncing a chain of mischievous deeds and all of them, feared to be caught in the process.

True.

Snehalata missed that point, what was Aparna trying to make after all. Aparna was right, if her father or older brothers caught her; they would be more upset with his belongingness than her ability to fall in love with someone of her choice at such a young age.

Aparna often said that her mother, was her support system, cause she was the one who not only nourished her but also understood what she wanted in life though sometimes she won't take her side due to her overpowering husband, Aparna's father.

Still, she had someone, which Snehalata was deprived of. After all, she lost her mother at an age of three. And, without her mother's support, she knew that losing him would have been easier than fighting for him with her own family.

Still, at this dawn of understanding, she understood after blooming in his love, all after accomplishing him as her own.

Though, Snehalata was beautiful, still looked average in comparison to her lòve, Alok. She had fish-shaped bleak eyes, straight nose, thin face, and dense wave like hair.

Her olive colored skin glowed through her petite physique. The feminine hormones of puberty had awakened her at various places like on an easel of plain canvas, as if, she was painted with deep brown, black, bright yellow and green like wild herbs.

Still, she wasn't the first one to be noticed amidst the crowd. Rather, he was Alok, who caught her attention and filled her all emptier parts with sparks of fire. He as usual focused towards his morning football practice.

There was a match on 24th between his school and Adarsha Vidhyamandir, located in Kakdwip. She noticed him as his gaze was still on that football, he was wearing a black colored half-pant and deep blue T-shirt while the T-Shirt had no printed words other than the word Captain written in bold, white letters.

Their school never had this concept of school dress, where unlike the western world the servers of school didn't mean to spread the message of freedom. Rather, this was an act to ensure that children from under-privileged background could afford education at minimal possible cost. So, children like Asim would wear the same pair of T-shirts in rotation at school as well as at home. While Snehalata could afford to wear A-lined tunic custom made from Kolkata for her.

'Are you staring at him?'

Before, she could even answer Aparna's question, one little smirk had already found a place near the corner of her lips.

'He is the captain right.'

Her words felt like she made a statement, rather than questioning her or she was trying hard to escape Aparna's question. That evening after returning home, she made a note and marked down the date, 24th March, 1986.

After all, She was a hopeless romantic in her expressions.

Next day, late in the afternoon, she was one among the crowd, cheering for her school, her football team, and Alok. As the entire school sat on the rough, dried up patches of dull yellow greenish grass. She was the one, standing, jumping and shouting her school's name to gain all of his attention. Her romance filled iris with passion was chasing her senior, young footballer, Alok.

As he ran forward with the football, overtaking his counterparts one after the other, finally shooting a long kick, and scoring a direct goal, she cheered in joy.

Alok wasn't new to her. She had heard about him from her people around and also from people who were not her family. Everyone was raving about Alok. Little was she aware that his mother was a close friend to her grandma, who stayed not afar but a few miles from Alok's place.

Plus, human connection among locals in G-Plot was stronger as artificial entertainment hadn't entered their lives like Kolkata. While, there isolation from the outside world, made them believe in their power of togetherness, whether in times of compassion or sorrows; they all were together.

During the festive seasons, Alok's mother, Pranati carried him in her petite arms, unlike the tree trunk arms of Hari. She would also carry few boxes of sweets or home grown fruits inside packets, which all along hanged from her other hand. While Alok rejoiced the taste of coconut desert baked, and in the end, sprinkled with palm sugar on top; this was Snehalata's Grandma's special recipe, which she would often make, whenever Alok would visit her place. All of this happened before Snehalata was born in that house, the house of the famous landlord cum businessman of

G-Plot, who had more assets in Kolkata than on this island, he took birth on.

All of this came to end after her birth, and the death of grandma, so various names never saw invitation cards from their home and few like Alok, reduced their frequencies of visit forever.

She loved gazing towards him like the bloomed sunflower moving towards the sunbeam's direction. So, she could bloom, and grow more until it saw its own end with the dusk of sun. Still, all of it happened from distance just like the love of the sun and the sunflowers. She would often witness him riding on his Baba's cycle while going back home, all not possible on those days when the celestial space downpour with all of its sweetness from above, to lift and sustain all those Sundarbans from the mouth of death. But Sundarbans have seen more harm to themselves during those rainy seasons, nothing like soft sprinkle to nurture the crops. Rather, those droplets would caress the little plants with love and roughness as passionate between two young lovers making love for the first time, consuming the other's wholeness without the feeling of hurt coming in between. Love, all coming down to lust and sights of unexplored places.

While Alok would wait inside the school building for the rain to pass, to leave G-Plot and move ahead towards the vast sea of the Bay of Bengal, Snehalata would notice him from a distance.

She always made sure that her gaze never matched his, Alok's beautiful eyes.

Though, she was loud-mouthed, out-spoken but for all those moments when Alok was around her; she would lower decibels of her voice with shades of Victorian Moral sensibilities and soft demeanor of mannerism. Especially, those times when he stood just few inches away from her, circling butterflies within her flat petite stomach. Still, as soon as he unlocked his bicycle lock, self-paddled to take a sharp turn and move past her, she felt the pain, the fear of not getting reciprocated being the other one, not the one. Wasn't it safe to love him from a distance?

The soft joys within her would feel the pleasure of imagining, he felt the same. Rather, than knowing the truth that he never felt for her, nor she ever existed for him. After all, the little things humans can't attain in this life or the lives they have lived before, they crave most for it. And, Snehalata was one among them. Until, two years of age, she would cling to her mother's cellulite filled breasts as her own cotton stuffed side pillow, and sucked every drop of milk coming out of her. Sadly, she was three, when her mother died, leaving her and the love and care she deserved back on Earth. Still, her family portrait hung on the bedroom wall, where her spiral curled hair falling on her face, dangling loose near her eyes, on her cheeks, and all over her face could be seen as she laid naked on her mother's lap as a six months old. She would complain on her adolescent days about why she wasn't made to wear proper clothes?

This portrait always remained her favorite. It always reminded her of her mother, but this feeling of abandonment scared her to get after one more chase after Alok.

Snehalata's first word was, Mamoni, sweetest version of calling mother in Bengali that too at an age where words rambled even before leaving the tongue. She was solely left with her hypothetical mothers, her two talkative elder sisters and one pansy sister-in-law, along with numerous brothers to take care of her but still nothing could replace her mother.

Her side-pillow, her mother was gone the day, her little brother was born. She would often blame him, the reason behind her mother's death.

Still, she knew, her Baba was right, how can you blame him? He was an innocent reason behind her mother's death. Few months after her death, both of them slept with each other, brother and sister with each other's leg intertwined with another. Finally, she became his mother and he found replacement of a mother in her; a mother whose blood was running inside him but not along with him.

'Will you accompany me till the river basin?'

'Around what time?' Aparna enquired with curiousness.

'Around five in the evening.' She spoke to her with as much sweetness possible in her voice as she needed her this day.

Aparna's eyes were looking here and there, which tried to avoid direct proper contact with her. She wasn't ready to say yes, yet couldn't leave her alone to wander.

'Did you hear that the big-mouthed crocodile caught Ananto's eldest son, Asim, and tore him into pieces within pool of his own red blood? While he alike his father, was catching Baby Tiger Prawns with his dip net near the river basin. He knew how to catch those fresh black striped prawns, still didn't understand the reflection of water, the movement of sea to ascertain the approaching danger like his father.

Do you really want to go there?'

She agreed.

'In case, my mother finds out that you and I, both were sitting on the lower sand-built ridge next to the earth brown mouth of South Sunderganj. The crocodile might spare me, but my mother won't.'

'Can't you think anything positive, less negative or not at all negative maybe?' This time a fierced voice of Snehalata was more demanding than before.

Believe me, I can, though not outside but inside the fat bellied crocodile. Aparna laughed as those words came out of her small mouth.

Snehalata smiled.

'Then, we both are meeting near the embankment next to the tailor boutique. See you around half past five.'

She walked away without waiting for Aparna's answer. She knew that without saying no, she won't ditch her.

The gleam of red burning sun was still visible on the waters. While the narrow sailing boats were arranged in asymmetrical line, a ruddy breasted white crane was jerking his sharp beak up and down as it tried to gulp the entire fish in one go. Along the same row a newly married wife searched for Red Hermit Crabs in knee deep water. All the while, waiting for the water to gush inside those little homes in high tides. So, the helpless crabs would come out to end their lives in her hand. The lower end of her cotton saree was soaked in water and mud-caked, still her hunger-filled dip net searched for more and more tiny red crabs.

Aparna was running towards her direction as she was late, the clock has already crossed six. There was no sign of movement on her flat chest. While her athletic legs paced with her long arms as she took large steps.

You found this place again. Aparna's overwrought words were struggling with her gasp for breath.

'Aren't you scared of your mother's presence, her Ghost? Haven't you heard your aunt saying it often.' Snehalata chortled.

'Fifteen years have passed. She might have taken a rebirth just like a daughter, like me. She might be blessed, pampered and adored by her mother. And here, I am still waiting for the old one, for her to return.'

'Do you remember the words of Grandma?'

'Whose?'

'Yours, not mine.'

'Grandma often said we shouldn't play here. Your mother has gone, now she will take you along with her.' Aparna added.

The amount of hatred grandmother had for her daughter-in-law, her mother, she would often take it out on her when she would scold and blame her but she reciprocated equal amount of love her to her grandchildren, especially little Snehalata.

But she never understood, whom to blame other than her misfortune. She couldn't blame her mother, who died in pain while giving birth to her sixth child, her little brother, Rahul. Though, the doctor had reached half way but by the time the doctor's boat found the shoreline of G-Plot, because of the over-bleeding she was gone. Was the blame of Snehalata's father, who listened to his own mother, who was reluctant to the use of a permanent contraception for her daughter-in-law?

Her Grandma might have never liked her, still didn't wish for her death, all was the fault of time and space as she was no different from all other Sundarbans' women. After all, it was his son's loss of manhood, which was curled between his legs. While news of modern science spreading her home, her land, G-Plot could perform surgical procedures to abstain his manhood and make her daughter-in-law barren forever. Then, how could she listen to his son and disrespect the culture, her language which taught her this?

Still, I came here, would come in future as well, amidst the smell of this loose alluvial soil that lies here with this smell. The heaven where her burned ashes and little chunks of solid bones found the place, deep brown Earth was the sole place of her existence. If not rebirth, these words remained inside her without any resistance to come out of her mouth.

Snehalata would often come here, but the frequencies of her visiting her mother's memorial increased with her age as she experienced more of this world, felt more pain and received more soft joys of happiness.

'Isn't this the same place, where you found the broken piece of your mother's nose stud?'

Snehalata analyzed the ground.

She nodded.

While Aparna felt as if an odd silence has fallen between the two. So, she digressed the topic towards her lover, Alok.

'So, he left for Kolkata. Did he tell you when he will come back?'

‘No.’ She replied. The silence prevailed.

After three and a half years

Her mind was adjusting to the space inside and out as she pushed herself out of the jam-packed metro. The crowd in front of her, felt like a bunch of mud-creepers, who were racing, moving in and out to reach back to its little home, hole. Finally, she found some space, less crowded during this office hour outside the metro station. The facade of station building read, Rabindra Sadan.

Though, she hopelessly searched for Alok, he was nowhere to be seen. Rather, fifteen minutes had already passed, and as usual he was late. The wait for him, made Snehalata anxious. At their last meeting close to the hustling street of Park Street, he promised to come on time in all of his future dates. But again this time much like all the previous ones, she ignored those vacant promises, the little compromises she made to adjust herself with him, and walk along with him. This was the first time, she was going out with him on a secluded date.

Both of them had exchanged numbers after Snehalata left G-Plot for her undergraduate education much like Alok. But, that was neither her or his personal number; it was the phone number of Snehalata’s hostel and the landline number of Alok’s owner. All this while, before she met him for the first-time outside G-Plot, she would send him letters from his hostel. Alok answered to all her letters. In few of them, he would admire her, compare her body to some art he read in an art magazine about which she herself wasn’t aware of. His writing sometimes enforced her to think, was it solely her body, her skin he ached for, or was it even her?

His written words would echo in her mind, and she would re-read them multiple times till she could memorize them in order. She was like the dark-skinned lady from the distant land, who waited long enough for her journey of armor to start. Yet, when it finally started, she realized he was the mirage, not the one she wanted. Alok was flirtatious, less demanding, and an expert in sugar coating the version of his words. On her initial dates, she mistook those words to be meant only for her as they had a gravity of their own. She was wrong, she wasn't special. He played with those words, with equal softness of heart with almost all girls like her. So, she envied all those girls, who shared a sweet polished conversation sprinkled with touches of flirtatiousness with him. But it was too late to leave him, feel less and think of sharing her other half of heart. Plus, she couldn't digest the fact of feeling judged any longer. All the while, she wished to stay along with him, where she won't be judged on the basis of her prettiness, something she was born with. Neither she had her hand in it nor wished to have. Rather, she wanted her vigor, colorful imagination to trigger pool of madness within her lover's life. She neglected all of his biased conversations as closing some doors wasn't easier any longer.

'Why aren't you dressed up? Are you going to meet her in your house pajamas?'

This was Alok's new roommate, Amarto, a single child of the Darjeeling Tea Estate's manager. Unlike Alok, he had a slim physique, not muscular or having the aura that belonged from the Purple land, color for Royal. He would have never resided with Alok. It was all a last moment decision as he wanted to leave the restrictions of his hostel room, needed freedom like all young males of his age and here was Alok, searching for a new roommate to split his flat rent into half. Alok was three years senior to him, still his aesthetics of dressing sense and grooming oneself looked the other way around.

Alok gave a corner smirk and added, 'she is accustomed to me being myself.

She can change her mind in case you don't change yours.

Believe me, she won't, the moment you become one's habit, what you do and whosoever you actually are, the person with her vulnerable condition tries to accustom to it. So, she loves me beyond these habits of mine.'

Amarto uttered no more words to prove him wrong. Just smiled and waved him goodbye before leaving their home, a small two bedroom flat before leaving for his morning classes in college.

Finally, Snehalata found a wooden bench to flex her tired legs. She looked lost between the unknown couples sitting on the staircase of the main platform, few were racing towards the cinema hall on Bose road, Nandan while their elbows intermingled with each other. She felt exhausted as she was going back to Sundarbans for a couple of days to meet her baba, returning from there the day after, and coming all the way to her college in Midnapur then to Kolkata. All this meant nothing to him. What if it did, or what if it didn't as an hour passed with him, and was nowhere to be seen? Though, the little pictures on the map couldn't define the time it took for the distance to cover a hundred kilometers from Sundarbans to Kolkata. In the decades that passed, the dinghy had got replaced with a steamer, which took three hours instead of half the day. But the local trains with its five hours travelling time was enough to break her down, burn out the last bit of vitality left within her. The weather was roasting and made her feel intoxicated with the heat above her head.

Midnapur had seen this heat earlier too, but being a suburb, the heat used to get replaced with soft drizzles of rain in the evening. All the same in Sundarbans, before the morning happened, sun showed its glowing face, night before the day the fireflies would fill the entire G-Plot with their green torches of fire burning within them, as if they came to announce the status of weather. Here, all of Kolkata seemed to boil without reversal signs of the dense water vapors, no one knew where they lost themselves. So, she searched for her plastic water bottle inside her handbag, instead a local brand of kohl pencil came out.

'Your almond eyes look more beautiful, spoke million unsaid words when you wear it on your eyes.' Alok had said on his last visit. This was a gift from him for the first time.

PARTED AWAY

Chapter 8

Hari reclined on his inclining wooden chair was calling for Pranati from his own bedroom. He called her name, again and again all along waiting for her to respond. But, he didn't get out of his chair to look for her. After a while, he thought that she might be inside the temple within the domains of their home, tied up in praying for her sons and daughters.

'Were you calling me?'

Pranati came from nowhere and stood beside him. She was clad in her plain, cotton saree, which looked unstarched due to the smooth lines, soft flow without crisps.

'Wasn't Alok planning to come back? What's the date?

Yes, he said on 24th August,' as the calendar showed the rest, 1993.

'Haven't you read his letter? I especially kept it beside your medicines and glass of water on this table.'

'I haven't taken the medicine, was reading this article on Bangla Literature. So, forgot to take my medicines. Don't worry, I will take it.'

Hari bent towards the table, not to grab the medicine but Alok's letter.

'You don't listen to me, then you complain that your blood pressure has increased.' Added Pranati before leaving the room.

Hari thought, just like him, Alok too would keep his promised words and come back to G-Plot, and teach the local students. But he hadn't stepped his foot here in the last two years. Last time on Shyama's marriage. Hari went along the hand-written lines. He was wrong, he wasn't like him. Finally, he was sure, he won't return and he again sank back to his inclined chair.

Alok had left Kolkata once again, but this time to go beyond the horizons he went to last time. He just like Hari would have got a teaching position in his own local school, with a pay slip coming to his doorstep in the end of month under the West Bengal Government. Alok was not the one walking on his father's footsteps. He was chasing for the one, he didn't have. It was his leaving his comforts or his ambitions to grow, be known beyond the land of G-Plot. For sure, he never considered staying back in G-Plot comfortably as he was searching for comfort, which he could find solely outside G-Plot.

But, Alok had always seen Hari's choice of returning back as his own comfort, which his young pumped up blood couldn't understand. He could never see that Hari's father was different from Hari, he would have never allowed his son to leave Kolkata for Delhi, outcasted him from the entire family and his home. While Hari would have different opinions, demands from Alok, still he would never force him with his demands, gave him a space. His father would have never given him, if he would have been at Hari's place.

While Alok lived with a greedy will within himself, he didn't feel satisfied with ease. His will forced him to fight with odds, so he would never feel like the half-filled glass. So, Alok booked one ticket in a general compartment, took some belongings in his tin suitcase, sent a letter back to G-Plot and left. Though, he wasn't one of the brightest, at least that is what his past academic records showed and left. So, he wasn't called to grab a luxurious position within a renowned firm. He just cleared the P.O exam for State Bank of India. He thought, he might get it. So, without giving much thought, he left Kolkata with all the cash he had. Probably, he had something else written on his lines of fate, cause the interview went well except for the fact all his answers were broken, mixed with partial Bengali and English, still factual terms and explanations were correct. So, when he exited the office at Connaught Place, he understood his chances were low, he didn't fit in here at least not for those officers. The next following days went on searching for new jobs, his new ventures for growth. Finally, he found two errand works to run for himself, one for his stomach and some to send for his brother and sisters. During the morning, he worked as a counter sales boy within a private firm while in the evening he taught lined-up batches of spoilt high school students in a Coaching Centre close to his place. His senior manager sucked his blood like a mean boss, where he would leave opportunities to take credit for his work, and seek out paths to pay him lesser than before. But life wasn't this hard when he first stepped on the soil of Delhi. His initial days before the interview went away comfortably as someone of his own, relative from his mother's side resided in Delhi. So, he took shelter at their place. While his distant relatives thought that he was going to leave soon, he was waiting for his result. His result never came and the currency notes in his pocket grew lesser in number. Once the known mouths now began to bite him like bugs, and jiggled like the coins as they spoke worst about him. They left no opportunity to make him realize that he was dependent upon them, that they were doing him more than a favor to keep him with them.

On late nights, he would hear their voices criticizing him, loud enough to reach his ear. This was on purpose. They all knew that they were audible to him, still the noises went on and on. Alok felt that self-respect no longer belonged to him, all gone with his departure from G-Plot. Up till one day when their noises and his agony filled pain came to an end. He was having dinner along with the members of his own.

'Are you going to get a job? Do you feel it's a hotel?'

Each and all words coming out of his uncle's mouth, his mother's second cousin pounced his throat, the food declined to go down as if a lump had formed near his throat. He could feel his heart racing.

'No, this can't be hotel. How can it be? Don't you get free food three times each and every day?' His uncle added.

There was no shame or embarrassment in his eyes. Alok's uncle seethed with anger and rage, the kind Alok had seen in the stormy waves of Sundarbans.

Mother was never right. She labelled these people similar to Baba or like the other people at G-Plot. Still, these words remained within him. He stayed not because of respect, rather the constant fear of losing the shed above him; the single shed which cultivated imagination of hope within him. On the next evening, when he returned from Hyatt Regency where he started doing some casual work a few weeks before, he found his improperly stuffed suitcase placed outside the main gate waiting for him to be picked and found himself a new home. The tin border of the case felt warm as if the entire afternoon, it was outside the house.

As he picked up the suitcase, he could hear their voices from the other side of the iron shafted door with rectangular iron mesh in the center.

'Where will he go? He is new to this city. Let him stay tonight. Its already nine.' His aunt was requesting his uncle.

'Don't worry, he is good at screwing other human's living as good.'

'But he is Pranati's son. What will you tell your sister?'

'Just that he was burden on our heads. We thought that he came here for a couple of weeks but it's been a month now.'

'He can go tomorrow.'

'No.' His uncle's decision was final.

Alok for the first time realized that there is nothing called as your own, your own blood, your own relative or your own love. Everything is a mirage; just a human belief to hold on to something. Believe in its existence to feel less alone.

The watch on his hand showed twenty past nine, but he had nowhere to go. His young blood was boiling. Trying to ask them for a respite for even just a night was out of question. Had he had to do that the last piece of his dignity left within him would have shattered into pieces too. So, for the first time, he didn't ring the bell and requested them, and left.

Should I go back? I already have Bachelors of Education degree after all I was qualified for a role of teacher in Sundarbans. Plus, my fate won't be that bad there.

He thought about all that he could the entire night while sitting with his trunk at the bus stand. Still, his words couldn't comfort his thoughts; his social consciousness kept stopping him. The fear of seeing himself as a loser in everyone's eyes was too much to bear.

'Finally, you have returned, you failure.' He felt no less than the fireflies in the Sundarbans, who fought the entire night for survival, name and existence and yet when the dawn came with the glowing sun, they escaped.

His mouth was smelling foul, his under eyes weighed with dark bags as he himself wasn't sure if he had cried or slept inclined on one of the rods holding the shed of the bus stand.

A pool of autos was standing, waiting to carry their regular customers on the known lanes and making way for the new ones. Finally, he left his seat, got up and walked straight towards the autos.

He paid him fifty bucks, and searched for random billboards which pronounced Coaching Centre. At one, he conversed with the coordinator, showed him his certificates and was given a job.

'Sir, can I get a few bucks in advance?'

'How much do you want?'

'Around one thousand', replied Alok.

'We will give you double the amount after one month, and you want halve of it now?

Your month hasn't started yet, you have just joined.'

He understood their concern, pleaded a little but it all went in vain.

'Sir, I might not come in the evening as I need to shift. But, from tomorrow onwards, I would come around the same time.'

After coming downstairs, he called a few of his friends from Calcutta University, who at present were living in Kolkata. While not all, few of them had left Delhi. Some invited him for lunch so he understood nothing more to expect from them, other than one meal. Finally, one of his batch seniors responded. Alok without any hesitance asked him if he could stay at his place for a few weeks. He was willing to pay for his rent, and a little more to put fire on his stove. Sometimes option creates gesture, values, and etiquettes within humans and people like Alok without options do what uncivilized and the wild ones do within an urban environment.

Should I call Sneh? His love had shortened her name from Snehalata. She was no longer her option, her choice or a single future unbroken or shattered amidst all of this.

Before leaving for Raunak Da's place, he decided to call her.

The line outside the P.C.O booth wasn't small as it was past eight at night. So, locals in huge numbers came to take advantage of the night schemes.

'Hello!'

'Alok, is it you?'

They talked for a while. Neither did he tell her about his new place nor about the lessening money lying in his pocket to have a rented accommodation of his own. How can he ask baba for his rent? After all, he did something, he was not supposed to do.

'When you will call me again?'

'Soon', said he as he kept the phone down.

As he boarded the bus, the crowded bus showed the pictures of shoppers returning after shopping in the market next to the bus stand. Ladies from west part of Delhi in their tight Salwar Kameez were carrying huge white plastic bags filled with clothes, and young college girls were sitting close to jobless young dates. While the frowning faces of middle-aged men reflected their pain as they would have preferred to enjoy summer nap on a Saturday instead of carrying baggage of their better halves without much choice, or options.

Once in a while between the DTC buses, one or two white ambassadors would overtake the over-bought Maruti 800s. Ambassadors weren't meant for the lower middle classes. In fact, it was the sole option for the upper rich classes, ministers and industrialists back in 1994.

The crowd inside the bus was giving him Habromania as he perspired standing next to sweaty, smelling uncles.

A kid stood next to his father as he held his own small packet of joy, his new clothes. Alok for a moment became ten years old, no longer struggling in his late twenties. Unlike, the little boy of Delhi, his father, Hari's condition was modest, just bearable to hold together four kids with food in stomach and education in mind. Alok wanted new pair of shirt and shorts for the festive season in October. So, his Baba held his left hand and took him to the cloth shop; it was a small room, which the owner has turned into shops. While the first floor was home to the owner, the ground floor was put out for rent, so little retail shops and local bank offices were functional there. All aligned in one row, grocery store for daily necessities, small stationary shop and few garment and mattress making shops from scratch were also there. The shopkeeper was known to Hari as he lived two houses down his lane to home. Whenever, people would pass across his little center of business, he would shrug his shoulders and flip out his lips at them. As Hari entered the shop, the place looked a mess with cotton sarees lying on the table. Not much was put into order after the departure of the last customer. The room smelt of dried leaves as those leaves hidden behind the racks of sarees and cloths made the insects not come close.

'Should I show you shirts? T-shirts?' asked the shop boy politely.

'No, I have come for Alok.' Hari smiled as he pointed towards his little child.

'So, Alok what do you want, T-shirt or Shirt? Whatever you want, tell me.'

The little islands in Sundarbans had few choices due to its remoteness, distance from mainland, Kolkata. So, by the time, the up-town fashion styles reached G-Plot, they were already outdated. So, matching pair of half-sleeve shirt and knee-length pants were common in inland.

The shopkeeper just had one helping hand, so sometimes in between calculating the cash, and billing out he would work as a salesman to handle the unmanageable crowd.

Alok would smile back at him as he would grin while showing him all he had.

Finally, the piece was decided as the discussion between Hari and the shopkeeper ended. Hari decided to go for the set, which was reasonable, plus its cloth material looked long-lasting. While Alok's priorities were simple, he liked the blue color and it had two pockets in the back side of the pant.

This one is for seventeen rupees, he said as he folded it part to part, then slid it inside the bag.

Alok remembered, his Baba didn't have the exact amount in his wallet. So, Hari requested him to write it down, and promised to return with the rest in the upcoming two days as soon as his income got deposited in the local bank. Finally, the shopkeeper took out his medium-sized, yellow paged notebook, which looked fragile with years of weighing down all the past bills, pending amounts which were recovered or the ones, never recovered back. Between this, detailed orders of cotton frocks and the new pieces of blouses supposed to be restocked, were also mentioned.

'Why do people come here when they don't have enough in their pockets to pay? Is this a charitable organization?'

Though, he mumbled those words to his helper standing closer to him. Still, Alok's sharp ears, born to eavesdrop, heard his cruel words which might have not reached Hari. Though, he was small, about to be eleven, still he felt like a metal nut was pushed into his skin, hammered till the red blood oozed out of him.

'Baba, I don't want this shirt.' He acted adamant.

'But you yourself chose this. What happened? Don't do this now, you have wasted mine and uncle's time.'

'Baba, it's not the design, I wanted. Let new designs come.'

While the shopkeeper remained silent and faked his smile towards his Baba as they left the shop without purchasing any pair for him.

'Lakshmi Nagar!' the conductor shouted.

Finally, most of the crowd along with Alok got down the bus.

HUMAN CONNECTION

Chapter 9

'Is it Alok?'

Raunak Dada hugged him as he welcomed him inside his small roomed flat on the third floor.

'Alok, this is your new roommate, mine from past four years, Shiva. Raunak's warm smile made him feel that few nights won't be miserable, at least he could sleep in peace.

When Alok called him the night before, Raunak who was sitting on his plastic chair for so long that his hips felt numb, collected his parts in together got up to pick up his phone. Alok had not known Raunak. Though, he was his senior, but in college they had never roamed, bunked classes together or shared some good memories, all they did was to wave at or greet each other while walking past in the college corridors. So, he just knew him without any kind of a judgement about him.

Though, he could have said no to him, but he couldn't as he knew the pain of loneliness, insecurity and all the struggling along with all the large section of suppressed masses brought. Nowhere to go, yet, nowhere to be.

The room wasn't enough for three, still the warmth was there, so was there home. One mediocre hall with one single washroom and kitchen attached to it. The hall was all the space, they had, to sleep, to breathe, to share each other's stories and to work on weekends. So, according to the room's size a single tubelight was enough to illuminate each and every corner of the room. While two beds were arranged next to one another, disintegrated, so you could see the two cotton mattresses covered with floral printed bedsheets. And, an extra pair was folded aside to cover their bodies, not from cold but the sharp stings of mosquitoes, which promised either itching, redness or diseases to end oneself. Raunak's bedcover looked faintly faded as the black roses had already turned into ashen, strokes of branches were missing, which weaved undistinguishable patterns.

While the sole source of ventilation for the entire hall was a large grilled window as the other two were obstructed by the sleek, shiny, metal colored steel almirah. There was a dearth of shoe rack, which Raunak and Shiva, both of them has transformed into front open wooden box meant to keep on the books. Though, the books were not plenty in numbers, but it looked stuffed by the way it was aligned while the visible particles of white dust creating layers and layers on top of it, proved that the house was of bachelors. Alok was given the plastic chair to sit on as Raunak and Shiva, sat cross-legged over the mattresses.

'You look fairly different, Raunak Da?'

Raunak shrugged his shoulders as Alok noticed that the fat round face was replaced with sharp notable jawline. He no longer kept the moustaches and beard, which he maintained during his college days.

All of it was gone, he was clean-shaven, and looked much leaner. But this lean look didn't make him any handsomer as the glow on his face, was gone along with it.

Alok, you take one of our mattresses with this bedsheet, otherwise you won't be able to sleep the entire night. Tomorrow we can go and purchase some mattresses and if possible one foldable bed too.

Raunak wanted to add on something, nevertheless he let it go.

I will give my share of this month's rent on 10th. Dada, is that fine?

Raunak nodded with an affable smile.

Within the following weeks, another mattress with a mustard colored mustard bedsheet was placed next to other two. The old, faded bedsheets of Raunak and Shiva, might have given feelings of discontentment if they were alive, after all those bedsheets had faded with time, age, and knew that once the days of the youth were gone, they were gone forever. While that night, Nakul lied with a level of satisfaction. He closed his eyes and slept.

Though, that night and the night before, everything appeared different other than the stars, moon and the moonlight that shone in the darkness, yet when he closed his eyes today he could weave beautiful dreams.

Things became better with his passing time, he had to pass through the storm and decide one of the paths, to lose or to win.

Until eight in the evening, he would take coaching classes then come back to Raunak's place, now his too. Though, on initial days, while coming back through the narrow lanes of Laxmi Nagar, he would mix up his routes, walk around in circle, until he learned to predict by remembering small details on his route in times without Google Maps like left to the Mango Tree standing on the center of traffic roundabout, then, right to the huge lamp post with specific advertisement to reach towards his destination. Still, his mind craved for reminiscence from past, his days during his stay in Agar Para, Kolkata back in 1989. Though, his stay wasn't long, still whenever he recalls, all the sweetness of nectar afloat back into his memories. During his final semester in College, he shifted to Agar Para as his allowance was cut into half. Plus, he could no more ask Baba as Alokesh got entree into one of the Private Marine Engineering Colleges. So, his donations ate most of Hari's saving, the one saved for Alok and his youngest daughter, the one born after Shyama. So, he started undertaking tuitions in his rented room. He would leave the comforts of his sleep at sharp six, to begin his timeline for the day. Then, clean the left-over utensils from the last night, take a quick dip, swim till another side of River Hooghly, and while going back to his room he would grab some puffed rice mixed with tangy yellow pea curry sauteed with sliced raw onions and green chilies, this was all he had in his morning breakfast. Before heading for a kilometer walk to reach local train station, change it in Sealdah, and reach Calcutta University.

He would always find something intimidating about these narrow lanes of Para. "Para" were the traditional Bengal's version of small colonies. Here, all the Bangla or Non-Bangla spoken communities, residing in West Bengal would join together to celebrate the festivities, fight with optimism to debate and discuss about political topics. All would share an intense desire to survive with enthusiasm. During the times of festivals. especially during Durga Puja, he would find nothing similar to Sundarbans except the Mantras in Sanskrit spoken by the Hindu Priest. Unlike, his home, the straight, broad alleys would be lined up with decorative bulbs, huge placards with the printed Goddess's face along the warm welcome note written in Bangla. The boutique chains will be competing against each other, giving new discount offers and three plus one schemes. Each Para in Kolkata, was just like one sole unit, one community, who would compete with other

Paras for the award of Best Goddess's sculpture, alluring marquee decoration or sportive activities.

While the marquee fitting in thousands of crowd within itself, looked like fantasy tales, were the traditional tent concocted out of Thick tent cloth spread over the four slit bamboo corners in G-Plot won't have given the artistic fell. The thematic based embellishment. Sundarbans was different, beautiful in its own uniqueness. The streets would become part of him as he would walk along with his college mates to reach the terminus, run his eyes through some beautiful girls, or enjoy his Adda on the evening tea stalls, where amidst endless conversations with known faces, all of them would rejoice the tea served in Mud Pot without handle with premium brands of Cigarettes. Everything was different, when he looked from outside, the face of Kolkata could never replace the Sundarbans, nor Sundarbans to Kolkata. Still, the warmth breeding in the hearts of Kolkata, the city of joy wasn't different from its home. Though, certain streets of Laxmi Nagar reminded him of Kolkata. Still, Delhi was nothing like Kolkata, no judgements breaded within them, nor the humans of Delhi gave them advices nor told them what to do or what not to do. After all, Delhi could never care for him, the way Kolkata would.

Though, Alok didn't like this new town, yet he stayed back, not for the faces, warmth or love, all for his ambition to grow. Though, life was better than before, he could afford a new place for himself, still he wasn't doing something great. Nothing permanent, strong enough to ask for Snehalata's hand.

He was Alok, living in future, dreaming about it piece by piece, and in the process, he suffocated his present little by little. What could he even do? How can he even relish his present, when it was neither admirable nor nothing was left to capture for a flashback. After all, it was longing for the light at the end of the tunnel.

Snehalata often said everything doesn't come to everyone with ease. Some are born with greater Karma to appreciate the present, behold it. Still, some yearn with longingness towards the unknown future. Dream, don't quit dreaming as human lives are embedded within the ecstasy of magic. And, you don't even know when things would change, change for better, and change forever.

And, Alok believed in her words, until the date his life took a U-Turn and changed for better, and forever. This was a Sunday Morning of 1996, when he got a call-letter for a permanent role of school teacher in a Government Aided school. So, in a moment of happiness, he decided to call his mother, Pranati.

Suddenly, the phone bell started vibrating, was it Ma's sixth sense, no, not possible. After all, his mother never called him, unlike the ways she would call his little brother, Alokesh numerous times each and every day. She would enquire about little details happening in his life like how he spent his entire afternoon? Does he need some more amount to survive amidst all the hardships?

Still, she would pick her phone, dial his number during her visit to Shyama's place in Kolkata. And, all along his sole pain was, she called to share her problems, the problems borne out of Alokesh and Hari's problem, not to hear his.

He was right, it wasn't his mother, Pranati. It was Shattered voice of Snehalata.

Sneh, where were you? Why didn't you respond to my repeated calls? What happened is everything..

She cut down his words with her own lines.

Baba has hitched my marriage.

With whom?

His name isn't important, she sighed.

For the first time, there was silence between two lovers. Both of them, were seeking for words, which neither came out nor eased out the torment between them.

Alok could feel his own breath, falling and rising with an unevenness of tides.

After all, this wasn't planned for you. What happened? What are you hiding from me?

Baba came to know about you and me. I don't know who told him about us, our love, and our togetherness of past five years. Alok, he sounded someone unknown to me, all of his words were twisted as if I, his daughter has brought dishonor to his home, couldn't keep my body and heart safe. I was at fault, Alok, I didn't listen to him nor allowed him to choose the one for me, shook him from his right and made him feel less of a man.

'Alok, this afternoon, he didn't ask me about my brunch or menu for lunch or about how my health was or how my studies were going on? I knew he was informed about us as he asked about you?

And, he didn't ask to know about you, rather to match that his heard words were similar to mine. The words weren't meant to come to a conclusion, provide solutions. It all went in vain in front of him.

His answer was simple, stay away from him, his and our families have differences, which can never be mended. Don't roam around with unknown men who are not yours. He said it is his responsibility to seek one for me.

Then he hung up the phone upon me.'

Even, Alok knew that meeting her father and asking for her hand, would be futile. He had his mind made up. It was not something he had decided overnight. Rather, this came with time, his instinctive reactions and her unbound love for her, his own Snehalata.

'Let's get married.'

'What about Baba? Won't I lose him forever.'

Alok could sense uneasiness in his voice as he framed those words.

'Sneh, neither you nor I have an option. We are constrained between the race of time, questioning ourselves all the while whether to weave the present societal image or fabricate our future together. Don't leave me alone like Ma.' He added.

'I got the appointment letter.' Said Alok to console her.

Still, these words remained unheard, meaningless to her. She was done. So, she hung the phone as she came on the verge of breaking down.

Snehalata was her father's favorite child as she was the one, who understood mother's love till three, then she was abandoned from it forever. So, her Baba became her father and mother. While his father kept a small passport size photo of her in his shirt's pocket, to remain with him, something of her during his frequent visits to Kolkata. All for the purpose of his own work.

It was a small passport size, black and white picture, which was taken in her fourth grade.

She knew, she was wrong. Still, what was right didn't come as an answer. So, she went with her instincts, being selfish for the first time, listening to herself and her heart for seeking her own happiness.

Next Week

Snehalata was sitting next to him. While the train was moving with calmness as it wasn't Superfast train like Shatabdi or Rajdhani. Still, the crowd inside these compartments felt civilized, adjusting and sweet enough to ask for food, which both of them declined. All along the train line, the scene outside felt sensual with scanty drizzle of rain. The palm trees were shooting high amidst the thick, lush green trees as the outskirts of Kolkata started. Alok looked towards her, there was moistness in her eyes though the tears weren't falling down.

Was she thinking the same as me? He wanted to ask her, not leave the question hidden, unspoken, but his mouth felt dried, and those words never left his lips. So, to start the conversation, he started with something unmeaningful, purposeless.

'What's the time?'

She looked at her metallic dial watch, where the dial was bigger than her small wrist. While the leather strap tightly clasped her narrow wrist as the insecure grip of Alok.

'Just five', she sighed.

The train came to halt for few minutes near the Bardhaman Station. The coconut trees were bending towards the curved tin shed of the platform, and shed's structure imitated the sharp waves of the sea. The platform had nothing much to offer except vendor's chasing the passengers coming in these trains, to sell "Mihidana", unique sweets, special to this land inside packed boxes. Alok's personal favorite was, has always been Mihidana, granulated form of traditional boondi, which means fine grained sweet made out of rice powder and saffron. During all his previous train routes, he would wait for the train to halt here, so he could get down and purchase few packets of this Bengal's sweet, all for himself and his aloneness in those trips. Yet, this day, he just watched the crowd in the platform, sitting next to her. He couldn't leave her alone inside the train. After all, he was scared of her innocence, which knew nothing about the destination, her new place, new home. Plus, he feared, she might breakdown and dismount the train to go back to G-Plot, her Baba, and he would lose her forever.

'Do you need water?'

She nodded. She was fine. 'Can I have something to eat?'

'Ohh! You didn't have dinner, did you?'

Alok felt guilty for not asking her before.

Alok ordered some food from the train's pantry. As Snehalata felt the unbearable heat, there were two fans circling above her head in slow motion. Neither of these fans, satisfied or comforted her tanned skin, rather they produced sounds disturbing to ears. The crowd inside her compartment, was by far large and Bengali except two women sitting opposite to her berth. The weave of jasmine, gold on neck and language they spoke, confirmed they were from Southern part of Indian Peninsula. Still, Snehalata couldn't make out, whether the language was Telegu or Malayalam. She was good at eavesdropping, so the sole word she could understand was about some place in Kottayam. The rest neither made sense to her, nor she took the effort to understand.

Suddenly, the conversation of these two women ended as one of those married women took out her lunch box, cleaned the banana leaf with bottled water and kept thick fold of newspaper below it to avoid litter. Alok seemed to forego the scenic view outside to concentrate on their plate, more out of curiosity than hunger in his stomach. The man and wife, with her sister rambled the broad grained rice with thick Sambar along with deep fried small fishes, and Thoran, veggies sautéed with crumbled coconut, which completed the platter as side dish. While immense satisfaction, feel of connection hit Alok as the man mixed everything on platter into rough ball with his palm, put it inside his mouth, chewed with softness and then started the process all over again.

After all, food wasn't meant to solely fulfil the hunger breeding inside human stomach as it talks about unknown culture, much relatable to Alok. While all along, Alok's mind cherished his thoughts of lunch amidst the land of Sundari Trees, his own Sundarbans, G-Plot. The smell of homemade clarified butter, boiled mashed potato with sauteed raw onion, spoonful of raw sunflower oil, sliced with green chilies. Still, the flavor intensified when its served with last night's cold fermented rice. Snehalata noticed Alok, he was making the man uncomfortable. Still, she felt deeper sense of embarrassment as the man's eyes met her, as if, she was making him uncomfortable.

She pinched him hard under his side elbow. Alok couldn't feel the pain, only a slight tingle to turn his face towards her with questions somewhere written on his face. Snehalata's eyes were big now, and somehow were the most beautiful look of hers. As her eyes were no longer sad, looking down all of her was looking into his eyes as his soul pierced with different range of feelings. He understood what her unspoken words meant, so he lifted his gaze from her eyes to outside through the simple, grey color painted iron rods.

And, once again his and her, outside were same, coconut trees, palm trees, and raw banana's hanging from banana trees. While the painted, red, bright yellow, blue picturesque houses were losing its identity amidst the lush green masses of trees. All seemed monotonous to him, though she was sitting beside him, he felt grateful that their separation in between wasn't for long.

Still, he could remember those days, when her father and older brother had come to know about him. All of them had brought her back to home. Her education which uplifted her also gave her the freedom to decide for herself and her family wanted none of that. None of his letters would reach her nor she could write to him. Meanwhile, her father searched for a groom for her, not seeking for the one better than she found for herself. Rather, men unlike Alok, who have belonginess from communities like there. So, men, who came to look for Snehalata, and find a bride within her, judged her for all see had outside. From long waist length hair to skin tone as beautiful as olive, all were observed in detail. After all, how can these men judge her as none of them has known her beforehand nor knew how she looked like beneath that olive skin. So, the sole means of judging in those arranged marriages with couple of meetings, was to grab whatever was visible outside.

'Baba, can you meet him once?' She pleaded. She wanted him, and that was her truth.

But none of those words reached her father's heart. Nothing melted within him seeing his own daughter like that. Finally, she did what was wrong, but then who decides what was wrong or right?

She eloped from her house, the one that no longer remained her home. While her nephew, not so young, enacted as if he was taking care of her and her responsibilities that afternoon, she managed to escape. On her route to bring college certificate, he dropped her in the middle to Alok. Though, none of his known faces, his own family members spared him and his newly created stories weaved out of a complete lie. Still, her nephew was brimming with happiness, after all, the last smile of her aunt before she left for forever, will always stay within him. Before that, was the last time, she saw the man, whose reflection she saw in Alok, her Baba.

That's how some things come to end, without meaningful conversations, and realizing how those relationships started in first place.

DANDELIONS

Chapter 10

Snehalata just like those Dandelions, had chased after her sun, Alok. Finally, she reached Delhi.

While the winter in Delhi, was nothing like the one she had seen in Kolkata or amidst the land of green Sundarbans. The temperature had dropped down to two degrees while the air outside was spreading chillness in winds.

'Alok, is this our home?'

Alok smiled back at her.

The house was nothing like her dream home. Small one room apartment with two little windows to let the air pass. A single mattress over one double bed, was all both of them had to share. Next to the bed, was a small stool and one broad wooden table. Neither the table nor the stool matched each other.

'Have I made a mistake? Was I bearing the fruit of not listening to Baba?' She couldn't control herself and longer and spoke those words to Alok. It was getting tough for her to contain her thoughts within her.

Her father owned more than a hundred bigha of land in total all around Kolkata and Sundarbans. He had built a home at least for each of his sons, and gold and cash for the rest of his children, his daughters. He had the power and image to settle his daughters with someone, richer, more successful in life. But that was not what Snehalata wanted. She had, and has always dreamed of marrying Alok in her mother's red Banarasi silk saree, all over spotted with Golden Zari in polka dots. While her Grandma's traditional Paati Haar, round Nath, Chik (choker necklace, and Tikli (Maang Tikka), all carved out of pure gold will be glowing like the first speck of morning sunbeam on her dull brown skin. Meanwhile, her baba, her everything, ma as well as father, will be standing next to her as the Shankh-dhwani (sound of the conch) begun. Ceremonies of marriage would refreshen the aura of the local Sudarbans, her own distant relatives, smile of her big brothers and excitement of maternal sisters. Yet, none of these happened as her Alok took him to one Kali Temple in Western Delhi's Tilak Nagar, purchased two long, white Tuberose garland from the corner shop just outside the Hindu temple, called few of his known colleagues from office, local priest and the registrar of the Delhi marriage office. That's how, she became his, married him and ended up coming to this one room apartment. Though she made sure, her and his stories never leaked, left those glass frame and portrayed as a memorandum of success amidst the ladies of localities, unknown old men who came along with Alok for her hand's tea, homemade Bengal's Trikon Nimki and collect their stories of new house and families back in Sundarbans.

Doesn't your mother visit you? I haven't seen any of your relatives coming to this house. Though, last month, Alok's mother came to visit all of you. Isn't your mother-in-law a bit apprehensive about Alok? Always praising and talking about her other son, the little one next to Alok, Alokesh.

Snehalata smiled. Nothing like that, she loves Alok with same amount of affection as much she does my brother-in-law.

So, her middle-aged neighbour couldn't reply any longer.

Alok's house transformed into both of their home, was located in Dabri, the South-West Delhi area, next to Janakpuri and Uttam Nagar. Often on her route to purchasing fish from the huge evening Dabri market for supper, she would notice those North Indian families on their scooters, where the man of the house in his orange colored turban would be riding the vehicle as his entire family, his wife, one or two little children fitted like a jigsaw puzzle in the middle. And, amidst all of these, the younger child would be entitled to stand in the footspace in the front of the scooter.

As if, the land we owned, wasn't enough to be divided among nations, states and localities, even those little barriers of class and existence for coins in pocket also came in forefront when you looked at the people around.

Still, Snehalata has turned this little, one-roomed apartment as her own home. The table and stool were painted in a shade of monochrome, the deep brown all by herself, then positioned near the bed. She also travelled the entire winter afternoon on her next day to Delhi, to find some beautiful outdoor pots from the nursery just fifteen minutes from her place. So, when she came that evening, she didn't come alone, two to three Montana bowl shaped pot along with rose, orange marigold, pink peony, all came along with her. Few aluminum pots and pan, plastic soap cases, White flowy curtains with beautiful drapes attached to it. The last item was heavier than all those items she carried all by herself, the long mirror to give her head to toe appearance as would drape her sarees. So, she paid few extra bucks to the Auto Driver and allowed him to place the mirror frame inside the right corner, just next to the brown stool.

After all, Alok started earning decent amount, yet, unlike her, he saved all for their future. So, neither those little pieces of art or those decorative house items caught his attention nor compelled him to bring back for home.

Finally, the almost new, pure wood sofa of their Landlords found a place inside that room. Though, the landlord wanted six hundred rupees for that piece as he himself purchased it for eight hundred, and hasn't used it for more than couple of odd months. Still, Alok and his bargaining power, reduced hundred bucks and paid five hundred for the same.

So, the house, which looked like a hungry tide beforehand, waiting to be occupied with more beautiful and pleasurable to the eyes item. All of a sudden, felt less hunger-stricken, more satisfied and obscuring with happiness as Snehalata and Alok, both of them, did their parts to the utmost level.

There entire day's routine was common, monotonous unlike humans who are blessed with opportunities, work hard in double times and create a life filled with passion, enthusiasm and challenges in their respective occupations on everyday basis. Alok would get up before Sneh, her hands still coiled onto his chest, a happy baby posture, go to the park in the backside of their Mother Diary, do some Yoga Asanas and come back after circling the park in stroll. Till then, she would have left her bed, freshened up and entered the open Kitchen to make breakfast and pack his lunch for the afternoon. Then as he came back to leave the home again for his office. She would indulge back in her household work, unpaid, yet, she was satisfied.

'Sneh, are those fried Nimki's finished?

You had almost more than half of the tin jar last time. Ohh! our next-door neighbor came in the afternoon, to see how we have decorated our new house and settled down. So, amidst few cups of milk tea with green cardamom pods and ginger, the left grams of Nimki's came to end.

That was their usual evenings, spending time with one another, sipping cups of coffees, complaining about the lives in this urban place, connoting the missing details of Kolkata and their Sundarbans.

Sometimes that's one of those beautiful facades of lives, the nine to five job, not good just enough zeroes in pay slip and comfortable lives with loved ones. They might have missed those fancy restaurant dinners in Connaught Place, late night movie theatres on weekends, yet, both of them were filled with gratitude of happiness amidst each other.

Back in G-Plot

"Did Alok sent any letter?", enquired Hari.

Pranati's answer was negative like all other previous times. But, all of us, you, me and Shyama has visited their beautiful place six months back.

Yes, we all did. Still, his presence isn't often seen, just like that blue moon which comes out and illuminate the sky and dozens of crowd below its shadow once in a while.

Don't you feel? Pranati that all of this would have been better, if he and Alokesh would have resided under the same roof, all in this house.

"Might be, might not be also", she replied. After all, two humans, who have same blood running within themselves might not have same opinions in their minds. The cut and cross, could have also happened between the two. They might have stayed close to each other, still their hearts would have been far apart.

After all, two narrow Sundarbans forest, running in parallel lines are so close, just a narrow channel apart, yet, none of them meet ever again once the creek comes between the two.

Plus, Snehalata's father is still filled with rage towards him.

"That's also true", Hari sighed.

Still, all these times, Hari wanted him to reside in G-Plot was all for him. After all, he was his beloved child, he was the one with whom Hari had more emotions attached compared to Alokesh.

And, then there was his G-Plot to him, he wanted to contribute more through his sons. G-Plot, the one below L-Plot, where river see its own confluence with the sea, the massive Bay of Bengal. While the sunshine glistens on water, sand and Tin Tarpaulin shed of local homes. As branched, segmented, ill-formed trees of Jhau, Garan and Sundari finds its place near the riverine. While its neighbouring places like Dhanachi, Kalas, Bonicamp and Bhagabatpur, are a concoction, formed and compiled to create Sundarbans, yet, differences lied in all those little islands. The soil of Bhagabatpur was home to fat-bellied Crocodiles and their respective kin. While Dhanachi was sole witness of white spotted deer, raising high, standing on last two legs to grab all the green leaves, their land has to provide. Then, there was Kalas, Deer also resided there, yet, the focus of this land was on the King of Sundarbans, the Royal Bengal Tigers who pounced, preyed and drank blood from the neck of those vulnerable deer.

Still, the land closest to G-Plot, where humans stories were heard and their existence was phenomenon, was L-Plot and I-Plot, both of them, shaped in those alphabetical letters of L and I as seen from the aerial view. After all, two islands can never have same stories to recite for chain of humans coming generation after generation.

Isn't land made out of humans, those souls resided, residing and will reside in those places?

When Alok was a little child, his Baba would tell him stories of Sabar Community. Sabar was one of those tribal communities, who could be differentiated from rest of the G-Plot natives through the dark-skinned color they bore as sun's gift, ate molasses of snails, deep-fried the salt dried fishes near the riverine embankment. While there children roamed and played with the sand in second hand clothes of other G-Plot's native. Alok has seen those boys, deep brown skinned girls, who neither went to school nor learned to read at home. All of those faces, seemed like a helping tool, who helped their parents to catch fishes, knit back the torn fish nets, cared their younger ones like mother of their own younger cousins. While Alok, Hari and Snehalata, chased for better things in life. To me, all those old Sabar womens, were more like African women back in European colonized periods. After all, till 1980s, these women worked as helpers in the houses of people like Snehalata and Alok. But, for what? Just two pieces of Saree in the end of year and meals twice a day.

Alok, when you come back from Kolkata, don't forget to do a little sacrifice for these faces of Sabar. Something, Hari all by himself, made Alok promise, before he left for Kolkata.

Alas! Everything gone in vain. After all, he never returned, and Hari could never see his little sacrifices for them.

That evening, one of Snehalata's older brother mocked at his father. After all, he was the creator of Alok, who couldn't face her family, or had the guts to do so. So, he eloped with their daughter. Hari thought of responding, but he knew the power of rage, which could never distinguish between right or wrong, could never see the cost of pain it inflicted in other people's heart. So, he remained silent, purchased few Calabash, diced pumpkins, small round potatoes the one which comes up with arrival of new season and some green chilies, and returned home. Yet, he never told the entire scenario to Pranati. After all, he knew the pain Alok has caused in her heart after marrying Snehalata. He neither informed her, nor took her permission. As if, he just said to share what he has done without feeling the need for her approval. And, Hari still remember that how after his news of marriage, tension in entire G-Plot, Pranati decided to marry off Alokesh as soon as possible with someone of her own choice. That happened, Alokesh had no women, whom he called his own next to his side, so he couldn't deny. Within next three months, Alokesh got married, but his own elder brother couldn't come back to see him reaching for another part of life.

After all, how could he? Accept his own Baba and Ma, all those communities breathing and residing in G-Plot including Sneh's Baba and brothers, were against him. Why won't they? He has married someone not his, not one, few classes above his own. When castes don't match, people with no credibility of their own feel like losing what all communities has secured for centuries as pride.

Four years have swiftly moved

Alok has stepped into his thirties, still his age doesn't show much on his face and hair, yet, black and lustrous with thickness. While Snehalata, five years younger to him, was beautiful with few pounds of weight lost near her waistline and face. Both of them planning for one child. After all, middle class families wanted their children to come out of the verge, come out of inflicted moments of saving amount for better things in life later on. Rather to come out of middle-class and reach the upper strata. So, unlike all of them, Alok also wanted to give them best education, less struggle some life and more opportunities that Hari couldn't provide to him due to his other four children.

And, amidst coming to new house, three roomed apartment with better facilities, decent neighborhood. He has left his Baba, Ma and Alokesh behind. The last time, he visited G-Plot was few months before getting married to Sneh. His own Baba, Hari grandpa has also come once few months after both of his son and daughter-in-law's settling. Though, both of them, persisted him to stay over for few months longer. But, Hari declined his offer and came back with Pranati.

After all, it wasn't like Hari has solely felt, Alok has also felt the distances born between he himself and rest of his entire members all tied under the shadow of same blood. Those roots, he has cut long ago, sometimes comes back in his dreams, make him repent for the losses, infliction of pain he has caused more to Hari than his own mother. But, once he goes afar, it's difficult to return back even how much you are attached from inside. The outer world sees everything on surface, nothing deeper, or all from the depth of an insider.

"Have you called Ma?", enquired Snehalata. There was no difference between his or her mother, after all she has lost her own. So, she called his mother, her own Ma.

What happened? Is everything all right back at home?

Snehalata took a long, deep breath. "Your Baba is no more".

All of a sudden, Alok could feel the floor below his feet slipping down. Was he suffering from some kind of illness? But, he didn't seem weak, at least not his voice when I called him previous night. Then, how come he left all of a sudden, unplanned, unpredicted or might be that's how vulnerable human lives are. So, for what, I was chasing all of these for so long. And, for the very first time, this came into his head. He felt guilt-stricken for breaking his promise, leaving all of them and merging, breaking and in the process constructing life, all for himself.

Though, he returned back to his own roots, all for a while, to prepare for the cremation ceremonies. The entire riverine was beaming with human heads, if looked from distance, all felt like little pieces of insects like those minute ants.

Finally, Hari's body shattered into millions of pieces, those pieces shattered into billion more crumbles to finally become the ash, the dust could carry.

About the Author

Ambika Barman is a 22 years old Indian Author, born and raised in New Delhi, India. She is a graduate in English Literature from Ramjas College, University of Delhi. Currently, she is a first-year MBA student at the Indian Institute of Foreign Trade, Delhi. She is a multi-dimensional personality- an avid reader, writer, trained classical singer and she also loves to paint and sketch. During her summer trips as a child, all back to her roots in the G-Plot, Sundarbans, she had heard and gathered all these stories from her grandparents, and locals which she has weaved together in this story. This is her debut novel, where she has written about all those people, staying, breathing and residing in the mysterious green land.